Dedication

For my three children, Jamie, Tamzin and Ethan.
Thank you for the adventure of fatherhood.

Acknowledgements

A huge thank you to everyone at The O'Brien Press,
especially my editor, Helen Carr, and designer, Emma
Byrne.
Thanks also to Oisín McGann, whose map of Habilon is a
true work of art.
Thanks to all the booksellers, librarians, teachers and readers
who support my work.
Finally, as always, the biggest thanks goes to my wife,
Mandy, for her unrivalled belief and encouragement.

Contents

Beyond
The
Cherry
Tree

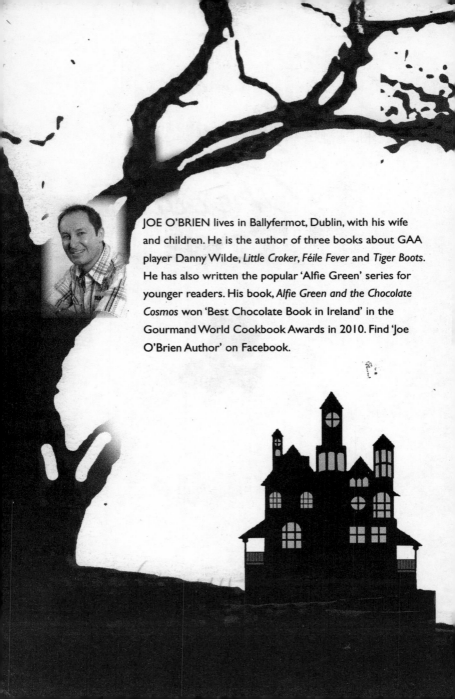

JOE O'BRIEN lives in Ballyfermot, Dublin, with his wife and children. He is the author of three books about GAA player Danny Wilde, *Little Croker*, *Féile Fever* and *Tiger Boots*. He has also written the popular 'Alfie Green' series for younger readers. His book, *Alfie Green and the Chocolate Cosmos* won 'Best Chocolate Book in Ireland' in the Gourmand World Cookbook Awards in 2010. Find 'Joe O'Brien Author' on Facebook.

Beyond The Cherry Tree

THE O'BRIEN PRESS
DUBLIN

Joe O'Brien

First published 2011 by The O'Brien Press Ltd,
12 Terenure Road East,
Rathgar,
Dublin 6,
Ireland.
Tel: +353 1 4923333;
Fax: +353 1 4922777
E-mail: books@obrien.ie
Website: www.obrien.ie

ISBN: 978-1-84717-212-9
Text © copyright Joe O'Brien 2011
Copyright for typesetting, layout, editing, design
© The O'Brien Press Ltd
Map by Oisín McGann.

British Library Cataloguing-in-Publication Data
A catalogue record for this title is available from the British Library

1 2 3 4 5 6 7 8
11 12 13 14 15

The O'Brien Press receives assistance from

Printed and bound by CPI Cox and Wyman Ltd
The paper used in this book is produced using pulp from managed forests

Chapter 1

The Blooms

Josh Bloom loved stories – all kinds of stories – but most of all he loved to hear the stories that his Uncle Henry told him about a general named Edgar Pennington. Most evenings, when Henry came in from work he barely had time to hang his coat up and untie his shoe laces before Josh pulled a stool over to the fire and sat eagerly waiting to hear which of the general's great adventures Henry would share with him this time.

'Have I ever told you about the time the general fell into the serpent's pit?' asked Henry, with a little lift of his left brow.

Josh's eyes widened.

'No, Henry!' he gasped.

Just as Henry sat forward in his chair to begin the story, Josh's Aunt Nell came in from the kitchen.

'There's a hot meal for both of you on the table, if you're

interested. That's if you're not too busy filling the boy's head with yet another one of your silly stories.'

Josh smiled at his aunt.

'They're not silly, Nell. The general was a great adventurer – the greatest. Isn't that right, Henry?'

Henry looked at Josh with both brows raised. He knew that Nell didn't really approve of his stories, no matter how exciting they were.

'Let's go and have dinner,' he suggested. Then he leaned a little closer to Josh and winked, 'Your aunt Nell goes to her club tonight.'

❧ ❧ ❧

'The stench was almost unbearable,' began Henry. 'As the general moved further into the darkness, the smell of death grew stronger.'

'Why didn't he try to climb back out?' asked Josh. He was engrossed in Henry's story.

'He wouldn't,' said Henry, while lighting up his pipe – a gift from the general, many years before.

'Why not?' worried Josh. 'I would have climbed back out.'

Henry bit on the tip of his pipe then pulled it away from his mouth and pointed it toward Josh, 'I asked the general that very same question, and do you know what he told me?'

Josh just shook his head.

'He said, "Don't be foolish, Henry, adventures are not for going backwards. Forward and fearless, that's the only way to find truth in one's journey."'

Josh felt a shiver rush down his spine. *I wish I had met the general!* he thought.

'What happened next, Henry?'

Henry sank back into his chair and returned to biting his pipe.

'He moved deeper and deeper into darkness until eventually the stench was so bad that it became almost unbearable to breathe – and then …' Henry paused.

Josh was hanging off the edge of his stool – the tips of his fingers were white from gripping the seat of the stool so tightly.

'What, Henry?' cried Josh. 'Henry, come on, tell me!'

Henry slowly moved his eyes toward the cottage ceiling.

Josh did the same, only swifter.

'What, Henry?'

'It came from above!' said Henry.

'The serpent!' gasped Josh, returning his eyes to the ceiling once more just to check that nothing was above *him*.

Henry nodded his head.

'Did he kill it?' asked Josh. 'Was it big? Did it attack him? Did it—'

Josh's frenzy of questions was interrupted by the sound of Aunt Nell turning her key in the front door.

Henry jumped in his chair. Nell was home early.

'Henry, what happened?' Josh persisted.

As Nell shook the rain from her brolly at the door, Henry made a move toward the kitchen door.

'Tea, Nell?' he called.

Josh followed Henry into the kitchen.

'You have to finish the story, Henry.'

'I will,' whispered Henry. 'The next time you visit me at work after school, I'll finish the story. But for now, let's just say that the general didn't kill the serpent but he left it with a nasty scar along the top of its head.'

❦ ❦ ❦

Josh went to sleep that night thinking of Henry's story. He rubbed his finger along a scar on his right arm, and even though he knew that he had got it from a fall when he was a baby, he fell asleep and dreamt that he got his scar on an adventure with the general.

He woke up the next morning still thinking of Henry's story, almost forgetting that it was his birthday – his thirteenth birthday! Nell and Henry were eagerly waiting for Josh in the kitchen, and when he walked in, Nell threw her arms around him.

'Don't kiss me, Nell!' cried Josh. 'I'm too old for that now.'

Nell wouldn't let go of Josh until she got her kiss. She was like that – the loving kind – firm and strict, but very loving nonetheless.

Henry stood up from the table and stretched out his arm.

'Happy birthday, boy,' he smiled.

Josh shook his uncle's hand.

'Thanks, Henry.'

Henry had a really proud look on his face, the very same look he had on all of Josh's birthdays. Josh always felt that Henry would have loved him to be his son; he never really questioned his uncle or his aunt on his past and his parents because he didn't want to make them feel that they weren't enough for him. But for some reason, maybe because it was his birthday, Josh felt the urge to ask Henry about his past.

'What were my parents like? My dad, what was he like? Was he like the general?' Josh smiled across the table to Henry.

Henry shifted his eyes to Nell as if to pass the question onto her. Nell began to fidget uncomfortably with the tea towel. Josh knew instantly that it was awkward for them, so he tried a different approach.

'Was my dad your brother, Henry? I hope he was.'

Henry smiled. He knew that Josh was just trying to make him feel good, but still he shifted his eyes toward Nell, who drew a deep breath, then put the tea towel down and crossed her hands on the table.

'I suppose you're thirteen now, Josh, and, well, there's no point in pretending that you're not going to be curious about, well, lots of things really.'

Nell was struggling to get to the point she was trying to make.

Henry decided to help out, 'What your aunt is trying to tell you, Josh, is that we'll always be here for you and you know that we love you very much, so you don't have to worry about anything like that.'

Nell interrupted, 'Just tell him, Henry.'

'Tell me what?' asked Josh.

'We've never met your parents,' said Henry. 'I mean, I'm not your father's brother or your mother's and neither is Nell, I mean, you know what I mean. I'm trying to say that of course we're your aunt and uncle, but we're—'

Josh didn't let Henry finish his sentence. He stood up and leaned over to his uncle and gave him a big hug.

Henry laughed, 'Whoa! Easy boy, these bones are getting old.'

Tears filled Nell's eyes, but she wouldn't cry. That was just the way Nell was – hard exterior and soft on the inside.

There was no more discussion that morning of Josh's real parents or even of his past, and he and Henry and Nell celebrated his birthday like they always did by letting him skip school for the day and taking a trip into the centre of Charlotty to pick out a birthday present.

Chapter 2

Missing

'Missing!' – that was the headline that leapt off the photocopied pages being placed onto every desk; the sun shone its blinding rays through the open windows of the Charlotty School classroom, illuminating the word.

Mr Higgins had instructed Josh to hand out the crisp black and white copies of the *Charlotty News* front page.

'I want everyone to look carefully at the heading,' Mr Higgins smiled excitedly.

Josh sat down, holding the last page. He ran his eyes over the large black letters that dominated it.

'Now have a look at the date on the top right-hand corner. Can anyone tell me the significance of this date?' asked Mr Higgins with a childish look of expectation in his eyes under their big, red, bushy brows.

Matty Baker was the first to launch his hand into the air. Mr Higgins hesitated before giving Matty the nod to answer.

'Go ahead, Matty.'

'It's tomorrow's date, sir,' answered Matty. 'Only it's twelve years old.'

'Very good, Baker. You can all put your hands down now,' instructed the teacher. Then he slid around his shiny polished oak desk on his bottom and began fumbling in his brown leathery briefcase.

'What's this all about?' asked Matty nudging Josh, who sat beside him.

Josh didn't reply. He was fascinated by the words on the page, almost as if he was falling under hypnosis with every line that his eyes ran across.

'Josh!' said Matty, trying to catch his friend's attention.

Josh jumped. Mr Higgins spun around again, holding what appeared to be an old newspaper.

'Now, boys. Following Mr Baker's correct answer, I have here in my hands the original newspaper of twelve years ago. Before I continue, is it possible that there might be somebody who can tell the rest of us exactly what this newspaper article is all about?'

Almost involuntarily, Josh Bloom's hand shot up.

'Ah! Mr Bloom,' smiled Master Higgins. 'You've read the article already. Good man. Stand up, then, and tell us all.'

Josh stood up and glanced all around the room, then fixed his eyes assertively on his teacher.

'I didn't read it all, sir, but I pretty much know the story anyway.'

'Really! Excellent. Carry on, then.'

'Well, sir!' continued Josh. 'I've heard it from my Uncle Henry. You see, sir, he works at Cherry Tree Manor. He's the gardener there.'

'Yes!' interrupted the teacher, wondering how long it would take the boy to actually get to the point.

Josh paused for a moment while looking all around the room again. He wasn't too sure about how much he should say, he knew so many stories about the eccentric general.

Some of the other boys began to titter.

'That's enough,' said the teacher. 'The article, Joshua. In your own time.'

Josh took a deep breath.

'Well, you see, Cherry Tree Manor is owned – I mean, *was* owned – by a general named Pennington. General Edgar Pennington,' explained Josh. 'And this article is all about his disappearance, twelve years ago, tomorrow.'

Now everyone in the room was paying attention, and certainly not tittering. They were paying attention because it was a mystery! Every young boy and girl loves a mystery.

And this story that Josh was beginning to unfold was indeed mysterious.

'Very good, Josh,' commended the teacher. 'You can sit back down now. I want everyone to read this article tonight, because tomorrow you are all going to Cherry Tree Manor on a field trip.' Mr Higgins could hear contented chatter ripple across every desk in the room. 'Now, boys. I know this sounds like you're all going on a big adventure, and well, I suppose in a way it *is* an adventure, but it will be a class trip and we will be there to learn.'

Mr Higgins looked over at Josh.

'As Josh has already informed us, General Pennington mysteriously disappeared twelve years ago. That anniversary falls on tomorrow's date. As a result of this, Claudia Pennington, the general's daughter, has agreed to open the house to various groups in Charlotty. And since Charlotty Primary was one of the many lucky recipients of generous funding from the general's vast wealth, Ms Pennington has kindly sent an invite for our class to visit.'

Unexpectedly, Matty Baker's hand shot up.

'Yes, Matty?'

'Sir, does the general's daughter still live in the manor?' quizzed Matty.

Josh didn't mean to answer on behalf of his teacher, but for some reason his mouth opened and words came out – loudly.

'No, she doesn't. Nobody's lived there in years.'

'Very good, Josh. You certainly have done your research,' smiled Mr Higgins. 'As Josh has just informed us, nobody has lived at the manor for many years, but it is kept in pristine condition, financed by a trust funded by the general's daughter. This fund pays for the maintenance and upkeep of the house and its many valuable artefacts, and, of course, for its immense, spectacular grounds, which Mr Bloom's uncle tends.'

Both Josh and Mr Higgins had captured the undivided attention of the whole class. Unfortunately for Josh, who was now bursting at the seams to continue the story about the missing general, a greater sound rang through the room.

The school bell!

In a split second, the powerful magic that mystery can hold was cast aside as the more powerful magic of the sound of hometime rang through the room. Books and pens were snappily brushed into school bags and thirty pairs of shoes clattered towards the exit.

Poor Josh's ears were hurting on the way home on the bus as Matty bombarded him with an interrogation of questions about the general.

'Go on, Josh,' hounded Matty. 'You must know what happened to the general.'

'I don't. Honestly,' insisted Josh.

'But your uncle's worked there all his life. Surely he knows what happened to the general?'

'Nobody knows, Matty. Haven't you even looked at the news headline? He just vanished one day and never returned. No body was ever found, so no one knows whether he is even dead or alive.'

'Amazing!' gasped Matty. 'Hey! Do you think we might find out something tomorrow, like a clue or something?' Matty's imagination was running wild now.

Josh laughed, 'I've been to the manor lots of times to visit Henry at work, and I've never, ever seen anything suspicious or come across any clues.'

Matty's eyes widened, 'Have you been in the house?'

'No. Nobody goes into the house. That's kind of why I'm amazed that the general's daughter is letting a group of school kids in tomorrow.'

'I'm telling you, Josh,' grinned Matty as he got up for his stop. 'Tomorrow's going to be a trip to remember.'

Then, he jumped off the bus, leaving Josh gazing back down at the newspaper article.

Chapter 3

Cherry Tree Manor

Josh was last to board the school bus the next morning. He was late – twenty minutes late – and he had to endure dirty looks from all his classmates all the way down to the back of the bus until he hid his head behind the welcoming headrest of the seat in front of his.

'What kept you?' tutted Matty. 'We were going to go without you, but I kept telling Higgins that you wouldn't miss this trip for the world. I think he's more excited about it than anyone else.'

Matty wasn't trying to brag for sticking up for Josh, but he was definitely making it known that he had stuck his neck out for his friend.

'Aunt Nell,' answered Josh, his face beginning to return to its normal sallow colour instead of the lush pink glow that had stung his cheeks from running so hard.

'Aunt Nell?' repeated Matty. 'Aunt Nell, what?'

'That's who made me late. She saw me showing the newspaper article to Henry last night and has been on my case ever since. She was badgering me so much about how I should leave Henry alone when we get to the manor, and not be bothering him that I ran out without my journal and pen. I had to go back for them. That's why I'm late.'

'Oh!' chuckled Matty. 'I didn't think of bringing a journal and pen.'

Josh turned and smiled at Matty, then rested his head back and stared out the window as the bus began to climb Gorse Hill.

It was about a fifteen-minute drive up to Cherry Tree Manor. None of the other boys on the bus had ever travelled up Gorse Hill – there was no need, as it only led to the manor, one road in and one road out – but Josh had cycled along its steep, winding roads whenever he visited Henry at work. He was familiar with every twist and turn and bump and hollow that the school bus struggled with as it slowly crunched along the gritty, narrow road that was cushioned with hawthorn and wild grasses and vibrant patches of yellow gorse in between. Finally, to everyone's delight, the rattling bus choked out a huge huff of fumes as it spluttered through the open tall black iron gates of the grand estate.

Josh leaned over Matty and raised his hand to the window

as he spotted Henry stepping out from under a mature rho-
dodendron bush that was beautifully covered from head to
heel in large spectacular white flowers. Henry was leaning
against a bench that sat beneath one of the many magnificent
cherry trees that lined the drive up to the manor. He lifted
his head and waved to the bus as it drove by, then, continued
to tackle a clump of cleaver-weed that had tangled in his
jumper.

All the boys on the bus turned and looked at Josh as if
to silently acknowledge that they had seen his uncle who
did indeed work at the estate. Josh blushed a little, but only
because of Henry's clumsy appearance; he had been fiddling
with his clothing instead of performing some brilliant gar-
dening task like felling a large tree or cutting the grass on the
big ride-on mower.

As the bus approached the house, it circled around a tall
copper fountain that trickled cloudy green water from three
dragon's mouths down into a large round pool covered in
duckweed. There was a small group of ducks swimming in
the pool. Their beaks were covered entirely in blobs of green
matter from diving under the water and searching for any
minute life form unlucky enough to please their appetites.
This was very amusing to all the passengers on the bus, but
the banter was quickly hushed by the voice of Mr Higgins at
the front of the bus.

'Now, boys, settle down. I know you're all excited and of course, so am I, but I want you to listen to a few things I have to tell you.'

It took a few attempts for the teacher to get total silence. Herding a busload of excited school kids on an outing is not as easy as commanding a classroom of attentive pupils in a teacher's natural environment.

'Good,' sighed Mr Higgins. 'Now, I want you all to be on your best behaviour. Yes, you're all very excited about this trip, but do remember that this is a fine stately home that deserves both respect and discipline. There will be a guide to take us around the house. I've been informed that not all areas and rooms of the house will be on show, so I don't want anyone wandering off. We'll all stick together as a group. And if you have any questions, leave them until the end, unless the guide says otherwise. All understand?'

Everyone just nodded.

'Oh! And don't touch anything.'

The bus emptied out quickly, until all thirty pupils and their teacher stood outside, gazing in awe at the general's great house.

'There's something spooky about that house,' sniggered Matty to Josh.

'Don't be stupid, Matty,' huffed Josh. 'It's …' Josh paused.

'What?' asked Matty.

'It's …' continued Josh. 'It's just perfect, don't you think?'

'Perfect?' repeated Matty. Then he looked at the house again. 'I'm not even inside and it's giving me the creeps already.'

Josh dragged his eyes away from the house for a second and smiled at Matty.

'Well, I think it's just perfect. Come on, they're going in.'

Cherry Tree Manor didn't have steps leading up to its front door. Instead, it had an unusual, sloped, winding, spar-kling granite pathway that twisted and turned around sweet-smelling beds filled to the brim with hyacinths, lavender and tall, bushy mop-head roses covered in small juvenile buds, which would soon burst out in welcoming colours. All the boys huddled in front of the two grand black doors with their gleaming brass knobs.

Then, almost as if the house had chosen its moment, the doors creaked open, and a small, slim woman in a tweed skirt and jacket with a folder tucked under her arm invited every-one in. Josh was the last person in line. Just before he stepped into the house, he turned around and caught a glimpse of Henry trailing across the front lawn with a wheelbarrow overflowing with cut tulips of all colours. Reds, oranges, yel-lows and stripy ones too. It was as if a rainbow had fallen from the sky and settled in Henry's barrow.

Then the doors closed behind him and, to his delight, the

colourful but ordinary world outside was gone. In front of his eyes appeared a much darker more thrilling environment as he gazed all around the fascinating and eccentric hall of the general's abode.

In an instant of stepping across the doorway, Josh felt something strange. It was like the house *knew* that it had visitors and it had suddenly woken from a deep sleep. Josh couldn't quite work it out, but he felt it – the house's energy, rushing through the walls and along the floor. He could hear the stretching of wood, followed by waves of draughts as if the house were breathing in and out. He began to feel less excited and more concerned.

Their guide in the tweed jacket, Ms Tredwell, was standing on the fifth step of the stairway in the centre of the hallway. At first she said nothing, but just looked around the gathering of boys. She occasionally fixed her glasses, which ridiculously appeared to be much too big to sit comfortably on her neat and narrow shiny nose.

She didn't mind the delay. All the boys pointed around the hall, whispered comments, and made exaggerated facial expressions each time their eyes feasted on something new. She expected this. You see, Ms Tredwell had done the very same herself the first moment she had stepped into the manor.

Finally, as it appeared that everyone was beginning to

settle, she addressed her tour, and as she did another lady appeared on the upper landing and walked down the stair-case and stood beside her.

Josh thought he recognised her.

'Good morning, everybody,' Ms Tredwell said with a hint of inexperience and nervousness in her voice.

As is typical of boys, nobody answered at first.

'Come on now, boys,' smiled Mr Higgins.

'Good morning,' almost everyone replied.

Ms Tredwell managed a trembling laugh, 'Well, I'm Ms Tredwell, and I have the very lucky job today of guiding you all around this – I'm sure you'll all agree – magnificent and fascinating historical house, which was once owned by General Pennington.'

She turned around and waved her right hand up to an enormous portrait of the general hanging on a wall of the first stairway landing behind her.

'He looks proper grumpy,' giggled Matty to Josh.

'He's a general,' smiled Josh. 'He's not supposed to look any other way.'

Ms Tredwell turned to the lady standing beside her. 'This is the general's daughter, Claudia Pennington, who has kindly invited you all here today.'

Mr Higgins began to clap and gestured to everyone else to join in.

Josh noticed the general's daughter looking toward him. He blushed a little and then turned his eyes away from her.

I've seen her in the gardens before! he thought. *Maybe that's why she's looking at me, she must recognise me!*

As the general's daughter returned upstairs and Ms Tredwell babbled on about certain paintings in the hall-way that the general had collected, all the class jotted down random pieces of information in their notebooks. Josh's eyes were fixed on the portrait behind his guide; he stared so inquisitively at the portrait that his guide's voice sounded muffled to his ears.

Suddenly he felt a shiver down his spine as his eyes made direct contact with the general's dark, glazy eyes. For a split second it was almost as if he wasn't staring at a mere paint-ing. He felt that the face was almost staring back at him with thoughts and judgements and questions of its own.

Matty was right! This house *was* spooky.

Josh tried to get back the enchanted feelings he had when he entered the hallway for the very first time. But then he noticed the ghastly carvings of small, winged creatures in the wooden architrave that roped around the walls of the hall. There were large, ferocious beast heads that hung above each doorway. These weren't the heads of lions or tigers or moose or other creatures that would be hung as trophies after a triumphant safari venture, but more sinister creatures of an abnormal ferocity.

To Josh's disbelief, among all of this extremity of the abnormal, dainty little Ms Tredwell had somehow distracted everyone's attention towards a collection of boring old paintings of horses and carriages and lakes with bridges and roaring red skies in the background.

Totally bonkers! thought Josh. *The whole lot of them. This is not what this house is all about. When is the real tour beginning? Why isn't she talking about all the strange things in front of everyone's eyes, the things that struck electricity into us all as we walked in through the doors? This house feels alive!*

Chapter 4

The General's Library

Josh elbowed Matty to get his attention and then pulled him aside. 'What's going on here?' he asked.

Matty just gazed at his friend, bewildered with his frustration. 'The tour,' he answered.

'Look around,' said Josh.

Matty did as Josh asked, then returned his eyes to his friend with the same bewildered expression as before. 'What?'

Josh pointed to the walls and to the doorways. 'Look, Matty,' he gasped. 'Have you ever seen creatures like that before?'

Matty just laughed. 'Yeah! In the zoo! They're only stuffed animals' heads, Josh. Look, there's a lion and there's some sort of deer, or something that kind of looks like a deer. Do deer have big horns?'

Kyle Thomas turned around swiftly to the two boys. 'It's

a gazelle.'

'Really?' said Matty. 'It looks like a deer.' He put his arm around Josh, 'Relax, Josh. They're not real.'

Josh just nodded, but he was secretly freaking out.

What's going on here? he thought. *Why can't they see, like me?*

Ms Tredwell interrupted Josh's thoughts.

'Now, if we can move out of the hallway and in to the main living room, I'm sure you will all be intrigued by some of the many wonderful artefacts that the general collected over many decades of travelling,' she instructed as she guided everyone to the far right corner of the hallway.

Mr Higgins turned around and gestured a *Come on!* to Josh, who was still standing by the entrance of the hallway.

'Coming,' he answered. The teacher headed into the living room shaking his head.

Josh was just about to follow when he suddenly heard a sort of thumping noise from behind.

He considered ignoring this noise at first, but his curiosity was now on full alert. He thought that this noise was coming from behind him; he felt sure that it would most certainly be of much more interest than whatever Ms Tredwell had planned to discuss in the sitting room.

He turned around and heard the noise again. He glanced over towards the doorway of the sitting room to check if Mr Higgins was looking for him, but Mr Higgins had obviously forgotten about him, and the door was now almost closed.

Josh heard another thump. He spun around the big empty hallway and fixed his eyes upon a door at the far-left side of the stairs. It was where he thought the noise was coming from.

This door had two signs on it.

A polished, small, brass 'Private' sign was stuck to the top panel of the door, and on the wall above the door was a plastic 'No Entry' sign.

Josh slowly walked over to the door, thinking that this must be one of the areas or rooms that Mr Higgins had been told was not part of the tour.

I wonder why? he thought as he carefully turned the handle. The door opened effortlessly. A library!

Looking over toward the far side of the hallway once more to see if anyone was coming, Josh stepped into the general's library, then quietly closed the door behind him. He stood in the centre of the book-lined room, his heart racing and his head light as the blood rushed through his veins with venomous speed. He hesitantly awaited the next thump, but there was nothing.

Was it all in his mind? Had the hideous creatures in the enormous hallway caused his mind to play tricks on him?

He began to turn around, gazing up at the vast rows upon rows of shelves packed tightly with books of all textures and sizes.

At the very top, almost touching the intricately cob-webbed ceiling, there were great big thick leathery books with their spines all engraved in golden squiggles.

The general must have been a very fast reader, thought Josh.

Suddenly, it happened. *THUMP!*

Josh spun around. He felt dizzy.

THUMP!

He quickly gathered his senses and looked down towards the very bottom shelf, facing him, near the floor.

Did I just see what I think I just saw?

Resting on the dull parquet floor was a small, thick hard-back book.

He turned his head to the side, just enough to read the title:

Beyond the Cherry Tree.

Josh knelt down on the floor and reached his trembling hand out towards the book.

He gently lifted the book off the floor and, as he did, felt a warm tingling sensation trickle through his hand and dart straight up his arm. Afraid, he let the book fall.

The instant the book touched the floor, it leapt up onto the bottom shelf and tucked itself back in between two bigger books, where it had previously been sitting.

Josh fell back onto his bottom and slid backwards across the floor, as far away from the book as he could get. He leaned against a row of uncomfortable books, but he didn't care about comfort – he was shaking with fright.

What's happening here? he thought frantically. *What kind of magic have I stumbled across? I've got to get out of here!*

Just as he was about to get up from the floor, he heard a voice in the room.

A man's voice.

Josh slowly looked up, but there was no one there.

The deep powerful voice spoke again.

Could it possibly be? the trembling boy wondered.

He hesitantly glanced over at the far wall of the library.

Right above a shelf lined with crystal decanters of whiskey and brandy and a small crystal glass sat a portrait of the general just like the one in the hallway, but smaller. Josh noticed that the medals that stretched from one side of the general's uniform to the other appeared to be glistening, especially the last one to the right.

Josh jumped back with fright, as the painting twitched its long curly moustache, and its lips began to move. Then it spoke:

'Don't be afraid to grasp your destiny, boy!'

What's happening? thought, Josh. *This place is haunted!*

Josh's initial desire was to get up and run straight out of the library. But Josh Bloom was curious, and it was that very curiosity that had lured him into the library in the first place. It was that curiosity that stopped him from running away.

So, very cautiously, he leaned over towards the bottom bookshelf and reached out one hand towards the book while trying his very best not to take his eyes off the portrait.

He held the book in his hand. No tingling this time.

He began to flick through its pages.

Nothing!

It seemed that all the pages were blank.

What kind of book is this? thought Josh. *Is it a book at all? Surely to be a book, a real book, it must have words in it!*

Just as he was about to put the book back on the shelf, it started to jump in his hands. It hopped from one hand to another and back again. It was almost as if he was trying to hold a hot loaf of bread that Aunt Nell had just baked.

Then the book just stopped, and its pages began to flick all by themselves, getting faster and faster and faster. The number of pages seemed endless. Josh didn't remember flicking through so many. Where were they coming from?

He held on tight as the book shook violently in his hands. He felt like the bones of his hands were piercing through his skin, as the whiteness of his knuckles gleamed bright through his flesh.

Suddenly the book stopped shaking and the flicking pages began to slow down; just before completely stopping, one page shot up into the air, gently floated its way down to him and softly rested on his head.

Josh let go of the book and took the page from his head.

The book leapt back into its place on the bottom shelf.

Josh watched in awe as the title, *Beyond the Cherry Tree,* slowly faded until finally it vanished all together from the spine of the book.

He felt that same tingling sensation in his hands.

He looked down at the page he was holding.

On the top of the page, glistening in golden words, he read,

'The Destiny of Joshua Bloom, Beyond the Cherry Tree …'

And, beneath these fascinating words, there were more glistening words. Just as Josh was about to read on, he heard his name being called.

At first he looked up at the portrait, but the voice wasn't coming from it. It just sat on the wall, not twitching and most certainly not speaking, just looking like a painting, as it should.

Josh heard the calling again.

It was distant, but getting closer.

He jumped up, folded the page and tucked it safely into

his trouser pocket. Then, very slowly, he opened the library door and peeped out. It was Mr Higgins.

Josh waited for a few minutes and watched his teacher frantically pace around the hallway of the manor. As soon as he noticed him opening the main door and heading outside, he slipped out of the library and jogged across the hallway in search of the rest of his class.

Chapter 5

The Riddle

It was quarter to eight and Henry was late.

Claudia Pennington had invited Uncle Henry and Aunt Nell to a special dinner at the manor in memory of her dear, long-lost father.

Henry was in the kitchen struggling to close the top button of his shirt, part of a most uncomfortable suit that Nell had rented for him.

Henry didn't like suits.

He wanted to attend the dinner out of respect for the general, but it was the whole fuss that was attached to the evening that bothered him.

Henry Bloom loved living by routine. Being a simple gardener was enough for him. It made him feel comfortable. Henry knew plants. Some would even say in the village that Henry understood plants and plants understood Henry, and that is why the gardens of Cherry Tree Manor were highly acclaimed from town to town for many miles around.

But now, on this very important night, Henry had to try and squeeze into this most uncomfortable suit that, quite frankly, made him look like an oversized penguin.

'Josh,' Henry called out with a hint of frustration and pain.

Josh was in the living room being lectured by Nell over his disappearance at the manor.

Mr Higgins hadn't fallen for Josh's story about being sick in the toilet.

'Josh,' Henry called out again.

'Go and see what your uncle wants,' insisted Nell. 'But I'm not forgetting about today, Josh. We'll talk more when I get home tonight.'

Josh ran into the kitchen.

'Yes, Henry?' said Josh, trying to hold back a smile as he watched Henry's face turn a hint of blue, trying to close his top button.

'See if you can do this last button.'

Henry sat on a chair and Josh tackled the button, thinking, *Should I tell Henry about the book and what happened in the manor today? Would he believe? Surely he would!*

Nell walked into the kitchen, her coat already on.

'All done,' smiled Josh. He decided not to say anything, especially in front of Nell.

Josh stood anxiously at the window and waved out, as

Henry and Nell drove off into the twilight.

He reached into his trouser pocket and pulled out the page.

Sitting on the edge of Henry's old armchair, he began to read the glistening words that riddled on the page:

Trail through the woods and a little farther,
Follow the silent path to the lily pond,
Stand beneath the willow that arches the water,
Take the golden branch and wave the Willow Wand.

'Pathway be there to the Cherry Tree and beyond'
You must say not once, but twice.
Be brave, young traveller, with your first step,
Without faith you will pay the ultimate price,
For to find your destiny
With the water, you must bond.

A mist will appear,
But do not be blind,
Listen and you will see,
Believe and you will find.

Before you awaits an adventure,
But one more task you must achieve;

Beyond the Cherry Tree you will travel.

To reach your destiny that awaits you,

Not only you, but others must believe.

Josh's stomach danced with all sorts of feelings: excitement, fear, happiness and confusion. They were all partying inside him, and this made him really feel sick. Over and over again, he read the enchanting words.

What will I do? he thought.

Up to now, Josh Bloom was neither adventurous nor brave, yet this page begged to differ. He paced up and down the room. This was indeed the strangest and biggest thing that had ever happened to him in his entire thirteen years of life. He thought about his life in Charlotty. It was sometimes a little boring and other times a lot interesting. But never adventurous!

Finally, Josh stopped pacing.

I'm going, he thought. *I have to go! But what about Nell and Henry? What would they do if they found out?*

His thoughts rattled on in his mind.

Why would they ever find out? he then thought. *I could just go and see, and get back before they do.*

That was that!

Josh put on his jacket, and grabbed the torch from his shoebox under his bed. He tucked the page back into his pocket and closed the hall door behind him. He ran around to the side yard and unlocked his bicycle, then cycled off into the darkness, heading for Gorse Hill.

Gorse Hill was no easy cycle, but Josh had cycled its steep roads many times before and that had rewarded him with extra-strong legs and excellent fitness. Fitness, however, doesn't help much on a dark journey and Josh was more than happy when the moon appeared from behind a cloud every now and then to highlight some of the many treacherous hollows in the road.

Every bend that Josh cycled around was taken cautiously as he knew that Henry's old Ford would surely struggle with the merciless hill and he didn't want to bump into his aunt and uncle. It had let Henry down several times before, and Mr Farrow would have to come in his tow truck and haul the car back to Number 7, Fennel Row, where Henry would tinker under its bonnet way into the early hours of the next morning until, finally, its engine would splutter a breath or two.

Josh sighed a breath of relief as the muscles in his legs once again began to relax and Gorse Hill levelled out just past the last bend. Straight ahead, he could see the old oil lamps on the two entrance pillars that had been lit to welcome the evening's guests.

As he approached the main gates, he jumped off his bike

and wheeled it around the back of a large cluster of neatly-clipped spotted laurels that gathered in groups on the top of a mulched slope, just inside the left gate.

Josh rested his bike on its side. It was well out of sight.

He kept his torch off as he walked along the near edge of the woods that wound around the left side of the manor. He could see shadows of people near the brightly-lit windows in rooms downstairs. As he trekked farther into the woods, he glanced back to make sure he was well out of sight. Then, with a sigh of relief, he switched his torch on. Josh looked back once more at the manor, then turned away and headed into the dark woods.

Every few minutes, as he ventured deeper and deeper into the woods, Josh stopped and shone the torch down at the page that trembled in his hand. He had walked a long way through the woods, and still there was no sign of the lily pond mentioned in the riddle.

He was quite familiar with most of the grounds of Cherry Tree Manor from helping Henry in the summer time, but he knew nothing of a lily pond beyond the woods. Henry had never spoken of such a place.

Still, he kept walking. It was a cold night and the crunchy twiggy floor of the woods was beginning to hurt his feet. All of a sudden, Josh was walking on softer ground. There was no crunching noise anymore.

He stopped and re-read the riddle.

Follow the silent path …

Josh walked a little farther. He noticed that everything was quiet now. No owls hooting from the trees. No badgers brushing through the ferns that lined the floor of the woods, and no crunching beneath his feet as he walked.

He shone the torch along the soft, thick, mossy, silent path until finally it led him out of the tall, dense woodlands and through a cluster of smaller, thinner trees that bordered the path all the way to flickering water.

The lily pond, he thought.

The full moon came out from behind a cloud to greet Josh and shine its light down on the pond, as if the dark sky had reached into its pocket and switched on its torch, too.

Leaning over the water in front of Josh was a large willow tree with no leaves. Its golden branches arched over the pond and glistened beautifully in the moonlight.

He slowly walked under the weeping arch of the tree and noticed that all the branches were golden.

'Which one do I choose?' he whispered.

Then, as if on purpose, the moon retired behind a cloud.

It was dark again.

Chapter 6

The Willow Wand

Josh started to wave his torch, bouncing its light from branch to branch, but still he noticed nothing special about this tree.

I wonder if the riddle is mistaken? he thought.

Suddenly, he heard a whisper coming from behind him. It came from the water.

He turned swiftly and dropped the torch. He knelt down and frantically searched the ground beneath him. It was pitch dark now; Josh had neither the light from the moon nor his torch. Then to his great relief, his fingers rolled over the torch and he grasped it. Just then, he heard the whisper once again.

Take the Willow Wand, were the words that waved across the water.

Josh jumped up, his heart racing and his fingers nervously twitching. He tried to switch the torch back on, but it wouldn't work.

Then, it appeared, right in front of his eyes.

He could see a glistening, golden, long, narrow end of a branch of the willow tree, slightly dipping in the water.

He walked over to the light. It was radiant and magical. Tiny bugs and insects danced in its light above the water and their reflections looked like magical miniature fireworks exploding up from the bottom of the pond.

Is that really a magical wand? he thought.

Very gently, Josh wrapped his fingers around the golden wand. It simply left the branch and was no longer a part of the tree. Standing upright at the water's edge, Josh raised the wand above his head.

At first he felt a little silly, doubting what he was doing.

I must believe, he kept thinking over and over in his mind.

'Pathway be there to the Cherry Tree and beyond,' he announced not once, but twice. He swiftly waved the glistening golden willow wand down and pointed it at the still water.

Nothing! Not a sound or a sign.

Everything was as before the boy had spoken.

This is crazy? I'm crazy! he thought.

Without thinking about it too much, tremendous courage came over him as he raised his left foot forward toward the water. He wasn't going to give up. He didn't want to turn back. He had come this far and he wanted this adventure, this magic, to go on. This had happened to him and it made him feel special. This was special. Something that Aunt Nell couldn't forbid him from doing.

Josh repeated the words through his mind, and then blurted them out just as his foot touched the water of the lily pond.

'Pathway be there to the Cherry Tree and beyond.'

There was no splash, no chaos, no dreadful disaster.

Josh's left foot stood firm on the surface of the lily pond as if it was on solid stone.

It worked! he smiled.

Quickly and excitedly, worrying that it might not last, he put his right foot forward, and that too felt like walking on stone.

The path was laid before him. It was a path of faith. Josh's faith, and he wasn't going to hesitate in taking it. One foot after the other, he walked across the water for a distance until he was met by dense mist which enveloped him like a blinding cloak of fear that couldn't be shaken or shed. Josh walked through the blindness for what seemed like ages. He could not see in front, behind, above or below and he was cold. He was colder than before and afraid. The sense of excitement, adventure, and jubilation of his achievement up to now was beginning to wane.

How long does this go on? he thought. *This is a very big pond.*

After such a long silence, he heard a noise.

Not a voice or a whisper like the one from the water, but a distant and faint repetitive noise, coming from the right, deep within the mist.

Josh stood still, his ears cocked.

What's that noise? he thought.

He turned towards the direction that the noise was coming from and started walking towards it, through the mist. As he got closer and closer, the noise became louder and clearer. Josh was beginning to think that he knew what this noise could be.

Could it be a frog or maybe a toad? he thought. *It sounds like a toad! Surely I haven't wandered in search of a toad?*

Josh was annoyed with himself.

I should have kept going the other way!

Just as he was about to turn back, the toad made a big, noisy croak. As it did, Josh found himself stepping out of the blinding mist and onto thick lush grass. His heart raced as he began to panic and he wondered if he'd gone too far.

Yet still he found courage to keep going as he thought of the general's great words in Henry's story – *Adventures are not for going backwards.*

He walked five steps, the flowery grass brushing his legs like a cat would brush against its master.

Then he stopped and looked up.

He was standing in front of a gigantic tree. Josh recognised this type of tree. There were many of its kind in the grounds of the general's manor. It was a cherry tree.

It must be the tree from the riddle! he thought.

Josh had never seen such magnificent beauty. This tree was quite different to the others he had seen. It was bigger. Enormous! And it sounded alive – just like the general's house. Of course, all the other trees were alive too, but Josh felt that he could actually *hear* this tree. There was a calming, humming sound coming from its trunk. Every now and then, a sudden adventurous gust of breeze would swirl through its leaves and Josh could hear the most beautiful and enchanting music echo from branch to branch.

This tree was so magical and here it was hidden away behind the mist that stopped at the water's edge, right behind where he was standing.

Josh looked over his shoulder at the mist. It hovered over the water's edge as if it was guarding the tree, protecting it from everything and everyone on the far side of the lily pond.

Should I go back? he thought again.

'Why me?' whispered Josh, looking up into the tree as soft petals fell from its flowers. They whispered soft answers in some language he didn't understand as they passed his face.

'This is not a question worthy of an answer on this side of

the tree,' said a deep, croaky voice.

Josh took a few steps back, away from the tree.

'Did you say that?' he asked, all bewildered.

First, there was a laugh, and then there came a rustle in the grass near Josh's feet.

He looked down.

Beneath him was a toad.

It smiled up at Josh then climbed its fat bulging body up onto a large mushroom at the foot of the tree.

The toad laughed again.

'Of course it didn't. Trees don't talk. But I am quite sure if they did talk, they would have very little to say,' said the toad. 'Mysterious and magical things are trees, but not talkative.'

Josh gazed in awe at the creature in front of him.

Thoughts filled his mind.

Where has this riddle led me? Where is this strange place of talking toads and stony water paths and things that just aren't real back home?

The toad smiled at Josh, widening his big bulging eyes as if he was expecting conversation.

Josh shook his head in disbelief.

'Careful!' warned the toad. 'Your journey has not yet begun, and disbelief only leads you down a short and regretful path.'

Josh felt his right hand tingle. He looked down and noticed

that the willow wand was glowing.

He had totally forgotten that he was holding it. He reached into his pocket and took out the crinkly page.

To reach your destiny that awaits you,

Not only you, but others must believe.

These were the last two lines of the riddle.

Is it really glowing or is it just the moonlight playing tricks on me? he thought.

'I must believe,' whispered Josh.

The toad perked upright on his stool.

Suddenly, everything flashed in Josh's mind like a memory that was real.

It is *real!* he thought.

Josh looked at the toad and raised the willow wand above its head. It began to glow stronger.

'I *do* believe,' he heralded.

The toad smiled, but shook its fat head and said nothing.

'I *do* believe my destiny,' stuttered Josh. He was trying so hard and yet the toad still smiled, shook his fat head and said nothing.

With one final burst of words from Josh, he waved the wand again and pointed it at the toad with great intention.

'I *do* believe my destiny is beyond the cherry tree.'

The wand discharged golden sparks that crackled through the air, and Josh fell back onto the grass, his whole body tingling from head to toe. He lay flat on his back, staring up to the sky. It was snowing petals from the tree.

When the tingling left his body, Josh grabbed hold of the flowery grass and pulled himself back up. He was soaking wet. He looked around for the toad, wondering what harm he might have caused it.

The toad was nowhere to be seen.

A cloud of sparkling, golden dust spun and danced over the mushroom where the toad had been sitting.

Josh was stunned.

What happened to the toad? he wondered looking down at the willow wand. It was no longer glowing.

The dancing golden cloud began to slow down and as it did, it grew larger and larger.

When it was about half Josh's size, it stopped spinning.

Then, it happened: it spoke again.

'You do believe, and so do I,' said a voice.

'Is that you, toad? asked Josh. 'Where are you?'

The sparkling cloud exploded and standing on the toadstool was a small, skinny and twig-like creature with great big green eyes and large round ears that curled towards its face. It had a flat stumpy nose that looked like Henry had just snipped it with his clippers.

'Who are you?' asked Josh. 'What have you done with the toad?'

The creature raised its hands in the air and smiled.

'I am the toad, but the toad is no longer me,' it riddled. Then it merrily hopped and skipped on the mushroom. 'It was a necessary disguise on this side of the Great Tree — always good to fit in with one's surroundings, although I take no pleasure in being a toad.'

Josh was confused.

'I don't understand.'

The creature stopped dancing and jumped onto the grass, which reached up to its ears.

It waved its way over to Josh and put out one of its hands.

'Bortwig,' announced the creature. 'Tree elf.' It smiled while still holding out its hand.

'Tree elf?' repeated Josh.

'That's right,' said Bortwig, moving his hand away. 'Tree elf or tree keeper or door master or ninth servant of the Great Tree after Hamvelin, number eight, who died at the young age of one hundred and eleven.'

'One hundred and eleven,' laughed Josh.

'It's not funny, you know,' insisted Bortwig. 'I'm one hundred and forty-two this year and not getting any younger. Now, are you going to shake my hand or not, Master Bloom?'

Josh reached out his hand and shook Bortwig's. It was warm, very warm. Much too warm for such a cold night.

'You know my name. How?' asked Josh.

Bortwig looked over his shoulders and became twitchy and uneasy all of a sudden.

'Another question not worthy of an answer on this side of the Great Tree.'

Bortwig turned and ushered Josh with a wave of his hand.

'It's time, Master Bloom.' Then the creature walked closer to the tree.

'Time for *what*?' asked Josh, with frustration in his voice.

'Time to go beyond the cherry tree, Master Bloom,' smiled Bortwig. 'Isn't that why you are here? Didn't you say that is where your destiny is?'

Josh walked over toward Bortwig.

'Why are we standing here?'

'Quiet now, Master Bloom!' hushed Bortwig. 'Great work to be done ... magic and stuff.'

Bortwig reached out his hand and touched the shiny polished skin of the tree's trunk.

Slowly, the gleam of the trunk dulled and a line of button-like markings appeared above Bortwig's hand.

As if he was tapping in some kind of code, Bortwig pressed his fingers randomly against the buttons in all sorts of orders, then stepped back. The buttons disappeared back into the tree and its shiny appearance returned. A knot fell from the tree's trunk, leaving a small hole. The skin around the hole began to turn in circles and the hole became bigger and bigger until finally it stopped, leaving a big, round opening.

Bortwig walked closer to the hole and then stepped inside the tree.

Josh didn't move. He just stood in front of the tree, mesmerised.

Bortwig's head appeared back out from the tree.

'Come along then, before it closes.'

'You want me to go *into* the tree?' asked Josh.

'Hurry, Master Bloom,' insisted Bortwig. 'You must go into the Great Tree to go beyond the Great Tree. It's the only way.'

Josh felt himself walking toward the opening and before he could change his mind, he was indeed inside the tree. He watched the hole seal itself and noticed the world outside the tree slowly shrinking and shrinking until it looked as if he was peeping out through a spy hole.

Then, it was gone.

Chapter 7

Bortwig's Abode

'Come along, Master Bloom,' urged Bortwig, ushering him in. 'We must get you dry.'

Josh was in no hurry to follow. He was too busy staring up at the unusual ceiling of the grand entrance hall of the Great Tree.

Joshua Bloom, to his knowledge, didn't know of anyone who had ever been inside a tree before. It was unbelievably spacious inside the tree, much bigger than it looked from the outside, and to Josh the ceiling was mind-boggling.

It was made of wood, as Josh would expect, but it wasn't flat or smooth like the ceilings of the manor, rather it was a maze of twists and turns, sort-of like the inside of a brain. Maybe this *was* the tree's brain that Josh was standing beneath?

Could it really be? thought Josh. *And where is the heart? Would I be able to hear it? Feel it? Is this tree actually alive, unlike*

other trees that don't think or feel or serve any other purpose other
than to be a tree?

'You'll catch your death, Master Bloom,' Bortwig said
with urgency.

Josh dragged his eyes away from the ceiling and followed
Bortwig out of the hall and along a long narrow corridor.
Just like the ceiling in the hall, the corridor was intriguing.
Its walls were not flat, but round. In fact, the whole corridor
was round.

Strangely, it appeared that the walls were moving, circling
around Josh as he walked along; yet, mysteriously, the floor
beneath his feet did not move at all.

Josh also felt like he was walking downwards.

This was making him feel a little dizzy, to say the least, and
he was finding it quite difficult to keep up with Bortwig,
who kept disappearing around bends.

Josh noticed pictures of creatures like Bortwig moulded
into the floor every time he came to a bend. Naturally, with
his curiosity, Josh would stop to look at each picture, then
realise that Bortwig was out of sight and he would run a
little to catch up again.

Finally, the corridor came to an end and Josh found
Bortwig standing in the middle of a large round room with
a sparkling fire behind him.

'Come in, Master Bloom,' greeted Bortwig. 'Over here, sit

beside the fire midgets, but not too close,' smiled the creature, pointing to a small three-legged stool.

'Fire midgets,' said Josh as he cautiously approached the ball of sparkling fire that hovered near the stool he was to sit upon.

'What are they?' Josh was fascinated. He squinted to try to see these little creatures within the fire.

'Are they dangerous?'

'They're tiny fairies that magically make sparks of fire when excited or angry or happy. Actually,' chuckled Bortwig, 'they just always seem to be making sparks of fire, and, no, they're not really dangerous. But they are feisty little creatures. Always fighting each other. The more they fight, the larger the fire and the warmer the heat they provide. They're the best way to warm the inside of a tree – real flames could burn the whole tree down!'

'Where did you get them?'

'They've always been here to warm the hands of the tree keeper,' answered Bortwig. 'They date right back to Grinif, first keeper of the Great Tree.'

Josh stayed close to the fire, rubbing his hands together while Bortwig disappeared out the far side of the room, through another small door.

Josh gazed all around Bortwig's room. It was very cosy for the inside of a tree, cosier than he would ever have imagined.

It had simple furniture: a chair with a small table beside it; a small bed in the corner; and some strange ornaments hanging from the walls.

A ledge close to the floor was lined with candles lit by fire midgets, as were the hall and the corridor.

'Tell me, Bortwig,' Josh called out. 'What's it like?'

Bortwig leaned his head around the doorway. 'What's what like?'

'Beyond the cherry tree?'

Bortwig's eyes widened, and a smile appeared.

'Like no other place you've ever been or even dreamt of being, Master Bloom. Beyond the cherry tree lies a land so wonderful and enchanting, inhabited by so many amazing and magical creatures, and peoples of great bravery and character.'

Josh was intrigued. Bortwig had made beyond the cherry tree somewhere he really wanted to go.

'I can't *wait* to see it Bortwig.'

As Josh's eyes almost completed a full circle of the room to where they had begun their journey, he noticed something strange yet familiar on the wall facing him. He stood up and reached out to touch it when Bortwig scurried back into the room carrying a tray with a teapot and two wooden cups.

'Be careful, Master Bloom,' warned Bortwig, placing the tray on the small table. He carried a cup over to Josh.

Josh looked at Bortwig, his eyes wide open. 'I know this!'

'You do?' smiled Bortwig, pushing his chair closer to the fire.

Hanging from the wall with its crimson ribbon was a bronze medal.

'I've seen this before,' insisted Josh.

'Really?'

'Yes,' said Josh, turning his head towards Bortwig. 'Where did you get this?'

Bortwig sat down and began stirring the tea.

He looked up at Josh. 'Sit, Master Bloom. Have some cherry blossom tea. It will give you strength for your journey.'

Josh sat down but he wasn't going to let Bortwig distract him from his interest in the medal by talking about tea.

'Where did you get it, Bortwig?' he persisted.

Bortwig looked straight at Josh, his piercing green eyes fixed upon the boy's. 'A friend,' smiled the creature. 'A very dear friend gave it to me before he disappeared a long time ago.'

Josh's face lit up. He looked up at the medal then back at Bortwig who seemed to be hiding behind his cup of tea.

'I know where I've seen it before,' smiled Josh.

'You do?' Bortwig placed his cup back on the table.

'In the portrait on the wall,' said Josh.

'Portrait? Wall? What wall?'

'The wall in the library. That's where I've seen it. It's pinned on the general's coat in the painting hanging on the wall in his library – the painting that spoke to me.'

'*Spoke* to you?' quizzed Bortwig. 'How strange!'

'There were lots of strange things about the general's manor,' Josh told the elf. 'It was very spooky. I could see horrible creatures and it – the house – felt sort of alive, like it was watching me, and not in a good way ...'

'Strange,' said Bortwig again. 'Very strange.'

The elf reached up over the fireplace, took down the medal and rubbed it fondly between his fingers.

'You know the general, don't you?' asked Josh.

Bortwig looked up at Josh, his eyes watery.

'I did,' he answered, his voice strained.

'How did you know him? ... Is that what this is all about?'

'What do you mean, Master Bloom?'

'All of this!' said Josh. 'My being here. You said the general gave you the medal before he went missing.'

'Yes.'

'Is he missing beyond the cherry tree?' quizzed Josh. 'Am I here to find him? Is that my destiny? Why was the general here, Bortwig? How did he go missing? What happened to him?'

'Stop! Stop! Stop!' cried Bortwig. He jumped up from his

chair. 'So many questions and yet we're still not beyond the Great Tree.'

'Won't you tell me?' pleaded Josh.

Bortwig leaned over and pinned the general's medal back on the wall, above the fire.

'Please, Master Bloom. Do have some tea.' He sat back down and began to answer the boy's questions.

'You see, Master Bloom, the general loved travelling beyond the Great Tree,' Bortwig began to explain while Josh sipped on his cold cherry blossom tea. 'Actually, you could say that he lived for travelling beyond the Great Tree.'

'Why?' Josh interrupted, slurping.

'Adventure,' smiled Bortwig, clapping his hands, and twitching his head in joyous celebration of the weirdest kind. 'And danger.' Bortwig's smile faded and his face hardened into a more serious mask. 'The general loved both, Master Bloom, and both are plentiful beyond the cherry tree. Indeed! It's true; the general lived a risky life on your side of the Great Tree. Many battles to his name. And when the battles were gone he had his hunting trips.' Bortwig paused, looked up at the medal and smiled. 'Oh, how he used to sit where you are now, and tell me great stories!'

'How did he go missing? What happened to him? Is he alive, Bortwig?'

'Alive?' cried Bortwig, his hands covering his face. 'I don't know. No one knows'

Bortwig's face filled with rage and hatred, and his eyes changed from green to black.

'Only one evil being can answer that question.'

Josh shivered, waiting in anticipation for Bortwig to continue, but he did not.

'What evil being, Bortwig? Who knows what happened to the general!?'

Bortwig clenched his fists, jumped up off his chair and angrily and rebelliously danced around the room.

This startled Josh.

'I can't. I won't!' raged the creature.

'Won't what, Bortwig? What's the matter?'

'I won't say his name. Not here. Not in my home,' insisted Bortwig.

'Please, Bortwig?' pressured Josh.

Bortwig stopped dancing, sat back on his chair and sipped some tea.

'Won't you tell me?' Josh asked one more time. 'Why won't you say his name?'

Bortwig drew a deep breath, and suddenly Josh could see the fury leave his face.

'All right! All right! I'll tell you' he agreed. 'But I hate him. I loathe him.'

Josh was all ears.

'Krudon, that's who,' snarled Bortwig. 'We were captured by him as he brought terror across the land beyond the Great Tree.'

'Who is Krudon?' interrupted Josh. 'Why would he capture the general? Were they enemies?'

'Great enemies,' nodded the creature. 'Krudon is a powerful and great sorcerer, but he is also the greatest of evil beyond the Great Tree. And he's not alone. He commands the goblin army of the lands north of Mount Valdosyr and he is master of the fearful and deadly dragolytes. Additionally, there are many others who are loyal to Krudon's evil ways.'

Josh felt a huge gulp in the back of his throat.

'Is the general dead?'

'I'm not sure, Master Bloom.' Sadness and a sense of guilt filled Bortwig's face.

'Something strange happened – darkness – great darkness. When I woke up Krudon was gone and the general was missing. He's never been seen since. I hope he is not dead, but only Krudon truly knows the answer to that question.'

Josh jumped to his feet.

'I've got to find him, Bortwig. I just know he's alive. I think this is my destiny.'

Josh couldn't stay easy now. He paced up and down Bortwig's living room, just as he did back home. All of a sudden, he stopped right in front of the general's medal and turned swiftly to Bortwig.

'What am I thinking, Bortwig? I can't go off on some mad adventure. I've got to get back home. Aunt Nell and Uncle Henry will be home soon. If I'm not there, there'll be questions, lots of questions, and I don't fancy giving them the answers you've given to me.'

Bortwig looked concerned as Josh bolted for the doorway.

'Wait! Stop!'

Josh turned round anxiously, his heart pounding in his chest.

'You don't have to worry about them, or getting into trouble. Nobody will ever know.'

'They will if I'm not there! I can't just go missing.'

Bortwig took hold of Josh's arm and led him back into the room.

'Magic!' smiled Bortwig.

'I don't understand, Bortwig. What do you mean, "magic"?'

'Master Bloom, have you forgotten what great and marvellous magic you encountered on your journey here?' asked the creature.

Josh shook his head.

'You've seen so many extraordinary things already, and yet you still doubt. The Great Tree is magic.'

Josh's eyes widened.

'Yes, Master Bloom! Magic that can stop all clocks from

ticking in your world.'

'But how?'

'Think now, Master Bloom. Do you remember seeing the petals falling?' asked Bortwig.

'Yes,' replied Josh, thoughtfully.

'As long as the Great Tree is in flower, then time does not travel with those who venture beyond. The tree alone is the same in both worlds — it flowers in both worlds, and those with the courage to believe can travel between the worlds while it flowers. That's how the general had so many adventures, travelling back and forth while the Great Tree was in flower, and nobody was the wiser.' Bortwig's head dropped. 'Until his last trip ...'

It was all clear to Josh now.

'So as long as the tree is in flower, I can spend as much time as I want. But what if the tree stops flowering in your world while I'm there?'

Bortwig raised his head.

'Then all clocks start ticking again. Every second beyond the cherry tree is a second away from home. You cannot travel through the Great Tree unless it is in bloom.'

'How much time do I have before the tree stops flowering, Bortwig?'

Bortwig shook his head.

'I can't be sure. Four, maybe five sunsets. The tree is already losing its flowers. I will know when the time is near, but that time is not now, Master Bloom.'

'I'm going, Bortwig'. Josh's mind was made up, but still he had worries.

'What if I'm wrong?'

'Wrong?' repeated Bortwig.

'My destiny, Bortwig. How do I really know if I'm right or wrong? I don't even know where to begin looking for the general. I don't even know where I'm going first. Tell me Bortwig: what lies ahead?'

Bortwig took Josh's hand.

'I will help you as much as I am destined to help you, but I too don't know the fate of the general or whether it is your destiny to search for him. But I do know one person who can help you find the right path.'

Josh's head lifted and his heart beat faster.

'Wilzorf,' smiled Bortwig.

'Who is Wilzorf?'

'A great wizard. Come, Master Bloom. I will tell you on the way,' instructed Bortwig, leading Josh out of the comfort of his cosy living room and out through another small doorway.

Chapter 8

A Vision

Bortwig told Josh about Wilzorf as he led him along a winding tunnel.

'The wizard Wilzorf was a great friend of the general's,' said the creature. 'He will have answers for your questions before you even ask them. I'm sure he'll be sending for us.'

'Sending for us,' repeated Josh. 'I thought we were going to see him.'

Bortwig stopped and turned to Josh. 'Nobody just goes to *see* the wizard Wilzorf.'

Josh shook his head.

'Nobody actually knows the exact location of the Wizard's domain. He has lived in isolation for many years.'

They continued walking, Bortwig upping the pace.

'Then how do we get to see him?'

'There's a place,' explained Bortwig, 'a place where you go

if you want to see the wizard. Once Wilzorf knows we are at this place, then he will send for you.'

'Then what?'

'Then you are taken to see him.'

'Do you think he might know where Krudon is keeping the general?' asked Josh, just as the tunnel ended with a large round door.

Bortwig turned. 'Don't get your hopes up, Master Bloom. Remember, I'm bringing you to see Wilzorf to try to find the right path. Where that path leads is not for me to say, but it may not lead to the general.'

He faced the door and stood in silence for a moment.

'Are we going in through that door?' asked Josh.

'Just a second. The door will decide when it is time,' smiled Bortwig.

As Bortwig spoke, the big round door began to slowly turn. When it reached full circle, Josh could see what looked like a shadow appear on the door.

'It's time, Master Bloom,' said Bortwig.

'What's going on, Bortwig? Why doesn't the door open, and what's that shadow?' asked Josh, glaring at the shadow, which seemed to mimic him.

'Don't worry, Master Bloom. The door will open. But not here, not yet. Soon!' Bortwig smiled at Josh then pointed to the door. 'Be brave, Master Bloom.'

'Not again!' sighed Josh. 'Why can't there be ordinary doors?'

Josh watched in anticipation as the shadow's hand reached out. He took a deep breath, and then bravely stepped into the shadow. Darkness like no other surrounded him. He could still feel his hand being gripped.

'Bortwig,' he called. 'Where are you?'

There was no reply.

Without warning, he felt his hand being pulled and before he could even scream for help he was flying through the darkness, freezing cold air rushing through his hair and whistling past his ears.

Then he found his voice.

'Aaaaaaagh!' he screamed as he swooped down, then up again, twisting and turning.

He felt like he was going to faint. Up ahead he could see a dim light.

As he got closer and closer, the shadow tightened its grip on his hand, until suddenly, they were flying over a field. Josh could see figures up ahead, but he couldn't make them out. It appeared that one was leaning over the other, with a dagger in its hands…

Josh felt a rush of blood to his head, his eyes were blinded by the light; he came to a halt, then everything went calm.

He could hear a faint whisper in his ear. Slowly, it got a

little louder and a little louder again until he jumped up and stumbled against a wooden door. Josh lunged away from the door, almost knocking Bortwig off his feet.

'Master Bloom,' called Bortwig, holding a candle in his right hand.

Josh shook all over and looked at the door in front of him.

'Are you ready, Master Bloom?' smiled Bortwig.

'I'm not doing that again, Bortwig,' he insisted. 'What was that thing, that shadow, and where did it take me? I was in a field, Bortwig, and there were other people there too, two of them, I think.'

'The black shadows are nasty spirits, but you travelled with a grey. It wouldn't harm you,' explained Bortwig. 'It was a vision that you saw.'

'A vision? But it felt real to me!' cried Josh. 'What was it for?'

'The Great Tree has given you this vision, Master Bloom. For what purpose, I do not know. Maybe it is part of your destiny.'

Josh was trembling.

'After you,' smiled the tree elf, pointing at the door.

Josh looked at the door.

At least this time it had a handle.

He bravely reached out, turned the handle, and opened the door.

Chapter 9

Arc of Habilon

A blinding ray of light shot straight into Josh's eyes as he stepped forward. Holding both hands up to his eyes, he sucked in fresh air for the first time since stepping into the Great Tree. All fear left him and he felt as if he was breathing comfort, familiarity and courage into his whole body.

Josh heard a loud slam and he turned around. Slowly his eyes found their focus as the blinding light dimmed. The door had closed and disappeared into the tree, leaving no trace.

Bortwig was standing in front of him, smiling and clapping and doing the strange twitching of his head in joyous celebration.

'Master Bloom! You've stepped beyond the cherry tree.'

Josh turned away from Bortwig, his eyes feasting on this

new world for the very first time.

'Welcome to Habilon, Master Bloom,' smiled Bortwig, 'the land beyond the cherry tree.'

Josh had never seen anything like this before. It was enchanting! Straight ahead were two tall stone columns that formed an arc. Great stone walls curved away from each side of the arc; on its left side rested an enormous sword held by a giant statue of a warrior, covered entirely in moss. This warrior was kneeling, but even so, he must have been ten feet tall. The warrior's right hand rested on the grass below, his palm open.

A row of similar warriors ran along both sides of the arc, standing upright and still against the walls with their swords by their sides. They curved around the lush grass on either side, leading back to two big stone tunnels where the trails disappeared inside, into great darkness, underground.

Beyond the arc were vast forests, and beyond the forests, as far as the eye could see, were snow-capped mountains reaching up to touch the skies above.

As Josh and Bortwig walked towards the arc, Josh leaned his head back and looked up at the giant statues.

'What are they, Bortwig?'

'They are the Zionn Army, Master Bloom,' explained Bortwig.

Josh stood in front of them, fascinated.

'Why is that one kneeling?'

Bortwig smiled. 'He is Sorkrin, leader of the Zionn Army. He is kneeling before the Arc of Habilon, waiting for his king to call upon his help.'

Bortwig pointed to the centre, where the two columns of the arc met.

'Do you see that centre point, Master Bloom?'

Josh nodded, his head stretching backward.

'That, Master Bloom, is where the king places the orb. On doing this, with his wizard by his side, the king can summon the Zionn Army to waken.'

'What's the orb?' asked Josh.

'An object of great magic, Master Bloom,' gasped Bortwig. 'He who controls the orb commands Sorkrin and his mighty army.'

Josh was now standing before the arc, right next to Sorkrin's hand.

'They're giants!' he gasped. 'But how can statues be an army?'

'The soldiers of the Zionn Army are made of stone. They stand motionless waiting for their king's command.'

Josh looked over to Bortwig who had just stepped beneath the arc.

'Who is their king, Bortwig?'

'Their king,' said Bortwig, 'is the king of all that is good.

The King of Habilon. Be patient, Master Bloom, for you will stand before the king and know him, and he will know you.'

'How?' asked Josh.

'Come along, Master Bloom,' said Bortwig, ignoring the question, 'I want to show you something.'

Josh, too, stood beneath the arc.

'Do you see that forest in the great distance?' asked Bortwig, pointing straight ahead.

'Yes.'

'That is Feldorn Forest, the home of the tree elves. My true home.'

Josh's eyes lit up yet again, as they had done so many times on this adventure.

'Are we going there, Bortwig?'

'Yes, Master Bloom, we are! There will be cheering on our arrival and great festivities.'

Josh could sense Bortwig's excitement at the thought of returning home.

'But what about the tree?' he asked. 'Do you not have to guard it? You said you were keeper of the tree.'

Bortwig laughed, 'I do not *guard* the tree, Master Bloom. The tree has great magic. I *serve* the tree and the tree does not want me to sit by my cosy fire-midgets while you seek your destiny.'

Bortwig led Josh down great stone steps, away from the

arc, and onto a carpet of wild, flowering meadow, which drew the eyes long into the horizon, all the way to Feldorn Forest.

'I'm hungry, Bortwig,' said Josh. 'I'm looking forward to the festivities. Will it take us long to get there?'

Bortwig shook his head.

'Fear not for your belly. We will not be walking.'

He knelt down in the carpet of white clover that hugged the ground beneath the tall wild grasses.

'Em, Bortwig, what are you doing?' asked a bewildered Josh.

Bortwig just waved his hand and pushed his ear into the clover.

After a minute of nothing, he stood up.

'Won't be long now, Master Bloom,' smiled Bortwig. 'He's coming.'

'Who's coming?'

'Our transport.'

Just as Josh was about to ask the inevitable question, he felt the ground shudder beneath his feet and he could see the grasses quaking in the distance. Josh stood back and stepped up on to the steps that led down from the arc.

'No need to be afraid of Mirlo,' laughed Bortwig. 'He has smelled me in the distance and now he is coming to take me home.'

As the rapid and vigorous flattening of the meadow flowers got closer, Josh strained his eyes to catch a glimpse of what strange thing might be approaching. Suddenly it was upon them and the grass no longer rustled and the ground no longer shuddered.

'Your transport, Master Bloom,' said Bortwig, pointing toward the creature, then leaning over and fondly stroking along its back.

The creature snorted and burped and exhaled disgusting wind from its rear end in its excitement at seeing Bortwig. It was like Bortwig's version of a pet dog, only Mirlo was no dog.

Josh held his nose.

'Uugh! What *is* it, Bortwig? It smells gross!'

'He is smelly!' laughed Bortwig. 'But Mirlo is harmless and has a kind nature. He is a glykos.'

'A what?'

'A glykos,' repeated Bortwig, climbing onto Mirlo's back. 'They're underground creatures that burrow deep beneath the soil for rich and tasty smaller creatures.'

Josh's stomach was starting to churn.

'They rarely come up to the surface,' continued Bortwig. 'But Mirlo is an exception. We've become great friends.'

Mirlo shook excitedly, almost making Bortwig fall off, then he stretched out a long sticky tongue, reaching it over his head to lick Bortwig's face.

When the tree elf and the glykos were finished playing, Josh climbed onto Mirlo and sat behind Bortwig, reluctantly holding onto the wiggly tentacles that ran along both sides of Mirlo's thick leathery back, just as Bortwig had done.

'To Feldorn Forest!' shouted Bortwig. 'Take me home, Mirlo!'

The creature's tentacles tightened around Bortwig and Josh's wrists and soon they were whooshed through the meadow. Flower seeds exploded past their heads as Mirlo dug his head beneath the ground and his two passengers screamed with joyous excitement at their exhilarating speed through the glykos' tunnels, heading towards the outer regions of Feldorn Forest.

Chapter 10

The Witches of Zir

Serula stroked her long, crooked, wrinkled, spiny fingers along the cat's black fur. It purred with contentment and lifted its eyelids halfway, revealing deep, fiery, red eyes that reflected the crystal ball sitting on its pedestal in the middle of the room.

'Orzena will be pleased on her return, my precious one,' screeched the evil witch of Mount Zir.

The cat paused in its purring. It growled in agreement, its fanged teeth stretching beyond its gaping mouth. The blazing fire in the corner danced and roared, then dipped and ceased momentarily before rising again. The cat lifted its head, then brushed away from Serula's hand and leapt across the floor towards the cobweb that veiled the hole in the wall opposite the fire.

Orzena was back!

A chilling gust of wind cried around the corner and disappeared into the deep crevices of the walls as Orzena scurried into the room, raging and ranting and hissing curses over her left shoulder. She was older than her sister and much more haggard in appearance. She was hunched to the point of almost constantly looking at the floor as she moved around.

But Orzena was neither slow nor ailing, and of the two evil sisters, she was by far the more ominous.

'I should afflict a thousand plagues back upon that scourge, for its misery far exceeds its usefulness,' complained Orzena as she pointed her hands towards the fire, drawing heat and energy and rage from its flames. Immediately, her eyes blackened and sank into their sockets, and the warts on her face enlarged and oozed poisonous puss that rolled down her face, scorching red tracks in her green skin.

Serula stood up from her stool and cast a bolt of crackling dust from her right hand towards the fire.

It exploded and smothered the flames, leaving nothing but ghastly, smelly fumes that circled, then evaporated.

It wasn't the first time that Serula had to break one of her sister's spells.

Orzena's face returned to its normal hideous appearance. The evil witch slowly released the fury from her body and once again slumped into her hunch. She turned to Serula and fixed her eyes upon her.

'Come, sister,' instructed Serula. 'Save your evil for a more worthy cause.'

Then she pointed towards the crystal ball and its cloudiness cleared, to Orzena's delight.

'It can't be!' she hissed.

'It is,' smiled Serula, revealing disgusting, rotten, broken teeth covered in strings of vegetable matter. 'It is the boy.'

'Are you sure?' asked Orzena. Excitement was rushing through her body.

'I'm sure. I've seen him and the tree elf walk through the arc.'

Orzena clapped her hands. Bits of wart-covered skin flaked and fell upon her cloak.

'We must kill him!' she laughed, snorting and scrunching her nose up between her brows.

'Yes! We must,' agreed Serula. 'And we must get word to Krudon.'

'Yes! We must,' agreed Orzena. 'We must kill him. It is Krudon's wish. He will be pleased, sister.'

Serula nodded her head. 'At last we will avenge our third sister.'

Orzena's face darkened again with fury and her eyes enlarged.

'She will laugh from her grave, her shadow will rise up from the depths of darkness and dance in celebration when he is dead.'

Then, once again, the fury left her. Serula scurried over to a dark corner of the room and reached out her hand.

There was a screech.

She pulled her hand back out of the darkness. She was holding a bat.

'You will deliver the message to Krudon,' she whispered in the bat's ear, holding it fondly against her face.

Then she held the bat in front of the crystal ball and pointed towards the image of the boy and the elf travelling on the back of a glykos towards Feldorn Forest. She placed her right hand upon the ball and began to work her magic.

'Image, I see. Image, I feel. Image, I take.' Suddenly, the image inside the crystal ball passed up into her hand.

'Through your eyes you will reveal.' She pointed her fingers at the bat and the image bolted through the air and pierced the eyes of the bat, where it remained to be seen by Krudon. Once again Serula held the bat to her face.

'Fly swiftly. Take this message to Krudon's castle.'

She held out her hand and the bat swooped out of the room, darting around corners until it finally left the witches' lair at the top of Mount Zir.

'We will send the scourge and two more,' insisted Orzena. 'As useless as they are, they will do nasty work on the boy.'

Serula looked over to the black cat. It was hissing and

The Witches of Zir

snarling and showing its fangs.

'Yes, my precious one,' smiled the witch. 'Gather two more and wait for us at the eastern edge.'

The cat raced out of the room.

'I will call for the scourge and two more,' said Orzena and she too left the room.

Serula and Orzena stood on the eastern edge of their lair, near the top of Mount Zir.

Snow blew hard against their faces and instantly melted on contact with their skin. They looked past Mount Erzkrin to the East and far beyond to Mount Valdosyr.

'They're here,' said Serula. The two sisters turned round. Standing before them were three cats.

Behind the cats were three goblins that Krudon had given to the witches as a gift. They were 'the scourges' – useless creatures, and a misery more than a gift. But Orzena knew better than to reject a gift from Krudon.

'Come forward,' instructed Serula.

The three black cats stood in line before her with their heads bowed and froth falling from their mouths.

She began her magic.

'Black cats of Mount Zir, rise up and be strong.' Serula's eyes blackened and enlarged. She pointed her hands towards the cats and wriggled her fingers with great intent. 'The gift of flight I give you, to quickly move along.'

As she spoke the three cats grew bigger and bigger until they stood large and beastly, high above their mistress. The fur on their sides stretched and fell to the floor. Wings burst out and flapped, then stretched above their bodies, ready to take flight.

Serula looked toward her sister for praise.

'Excellent, sister,' smiled Orzena.

Orzena approached the three goblins.

One goblin stepped forward to her.

'There is a boy travelling with a tree elf. He is The One,' the elder witch informed him. Her eyes again filled with fury, 'KILL HIM!' she screeched.

The goblin nodded, then grunted to the other two. The three goblins climbed up on the cats, whose wings began to flap violently. Serula and Orzena stepped aside. The beasts of Mount Zir raced towards the snow-capped edge and took flight, heading south in search for the boy and the elf.

The witches watched contentedly for a while before returning to the evil depths of their lair, pleased and eager for the fruits their witchery would bring.

Chapter 11

Feldorn Forest

'Look, Bortwig!' shouted Josh, pointing toward the evening sky. Mirlo slowed his thrashing pace as he approached the edge of the forest.

Daylight was quickly receding behind the distant mountains. Darkness had almost come completely when suddenly Josh saw a flash of orange soar over their heads and vanish as if the sky had swallowed it.

'They see us,' chuckled Bortwig. 'There will be great festivities.'

Suddenly, the black sky was blitzed with burning arrows. The sounding of horns followed this from the high tips of the outer trees of the forest.

Mirlo slowed down until he stopped where the tall grasses thinned beneath the moonlit shadows of Feldorn Forest. Bortwig jumped off and knelt down beside Mirlo's head, stroking it as the frightened creature wailed. He dug his face back into the ground, barely allowing his eyes to peep up at Bortwig.

'It's all right, Mirlo. Calm down boy. There's no danger for you.'

The instant Josh's feet touched the ground, Mirlo's tentacles retracted into his body. Then the petrified creature vanished within the depths of the soil, and was gone.

'Will Mirlo be alright, Bortwig?' Josh barely knew the creature, yet already Mirlo's docile nature made Josh like him and feel compassion towards him.

'Mirlo will be fine, Master Bloom. Worry not. We must go now, quickly. It's dark and they'll be waiting.'

The boy and the tree elf brushed their way through the dense, moist foliage that lined their path through the depths of the forest. Josh could barely see anything in front of him as the light from the moon above offered little chance or invitation to peer upon the floor of the tree elves' forest.

The only lights that caught Josh's eyes were tiny, green, flickering lights from the trees above.

They were random flickerings, coming from above and below and on both sides. They seemed to be moving at the same pace as Josh and Bortwig. They were always there. Never once since the boy and the elf entered the forest had the flickering ceased, not even for a short time.

'Bortwig,' said Josh. 'Are we being followed?' he pointed above.

Bortwig chuckled. 'I thought you were a little distracted. Sorry, Master Bloom. My fault. I should have known to tell you. Archers. Nothing to fear.'

'Archers?' repeated Joshua. 'The ones that lit up the sky and frightened Mirlo?'

'Yes,' answered Bortwig.

'Are they tree elves, like you?'

Bortwig stopped, and turned around to Josh, his eyes flickering in the darkness just like the archers above.

'Tree elves they are, Master Bloom. But not like me. Archers don't ever go where we are about to go, and they never ever leave the rooftops of Feldorn Forest.'

'Never?' asked Josh. He shivered. It was getting cold, and he was soaked from brushing through wet ferns and other shade-loving plants that lived and thrived beneath the dense shadow of the forest.

'Never,' repeated Bortwig. 'Not ever to wander, travel or explore.'

'Why?'

'That is the way it is. Archers are the protectors of Feldorn Forest and nothing else.'

Then Bortwig glanced above just once and ushered the boy onward.

'Almost here, Master Bloom. Now where is it? Always so hard to see in the dark.'

Suddenly, Josh could see flickering eyes peer around a tree.

'Bortwig!' he whispered. 'Bortwig, stop!'

Bortwig was busy looking for whatever he was looking for, but eventually he did stop and he did listen.

'I think there's an archer following us,' gasped Josh.

'Of course,' said Bortwig. 'There are lots of archers following us. That's what they do. Don't worry, Master Bloom. The archers are watching us from high above for our own good, not for harm or mischief. It is our leader's command.'

Momentarily, Josh wondered who the tree elves' leader was. But that wasn't so important right now.

'Not from above; from behind. I saw one watching us from behind a tree back there.'

'Really?' smiled Bortwig.

'What's so amusing?' frowned Josh.

'He'll never let me get away with this one,' chuckled Bortwig. 'Come on, then, out from your hiding and your mischief!'

Just as Bortwig spoke, bright green eyes peered around the tree and slowly moved towards Josh and Bortwig. Finally, standing in front of them was another elf just like Bortwig.

'Forgot your way back, Bortwig, tree elf? Has it been too long?'

'Never!' tutted Bortwig. 'Tigfry, tree elf, always the funny one.'

The two elves hugged, did the funny twitching thing with their heads, clapped hands merrily and laughed and hugged again.

'Norlif awaits, Bortwig, tree elf,' informed Tigfry. He looked Josh up and down with great curiosity and made strange shapes with his face.

This made Josh very uncomfortable.

'Who is Norlif?' asked Josh, trying to break away from Tigfry's stare.

'He's the High Elf,' answered Tigfry. 'He is anxious to meet The One.'

'"The One"?' repeated Josh. 'What does he mean, Bortwig?'

Bortwig scowled at Tigfry. 'Tigfry, tree elf, hold your tongue.'

Tigfry lowered his head. Before Josh had time to ask the question again, Bortwig was ushering him and Tigfry toward the tree that Tigfry was hiding behind.

'We'd better not leave Norlif waiting,' said Bortwig.

'Where is Norlif?' asked Josh. 'Is he hiding too?'

Tigfry managed a slight chuckle. Before Bortwig could scold him, he playfully suggested that Josh repeat a riddle after him, so that the way to Norlif would be revealed.

'Always playing games, Tigfry, tree elf,' smiled Bortwig.

Josh was a little confused.

Tigfry began to riddle.

This must be common with tree elves, thought Josh.

Blindness be gone,
Light dance all around,
Forest of Feldorn, open the eyes of those you wish to be found.

Tigfry tapped the tree once and suddenly a burst of golden, sparkling dust danced around the tree and climbed higher into the distant roof of the forest. Josh watched in awe as a sparkling stairway was revealed; it wound around the tree, rising and rising, following the magical dust.

'The way to Norlif,' pointed Bortwig. 'Come along, then!'

Josh began to climb, step after step, winding around the tree, following the two elves higher and higher as the magical sparkling dust led the way. There were more than just steps. Bridges and small dwellings formed in front of Josh's gaping eyes.

Josh noticed carvings in the wooden bridges, just like the ones in the cherry tree. They were of elves in battles with fearsome creatures – unrecognisable creatures to Josh – and there were various riddles scrolled into tall wooden posts.

Josh stopped momentarily to read one of the riddles –

See them come
March through the night

Songs will be sung
From dark until light

All Elves are brave
All Elves will fight

Feldorn we save
From dark evil blight

'Come along then,' said Tigfry.

More tree elves appeared, too, from around corners, out of windows and on branches. From clusters of thick green foliage, eyes peered in one direction: toward the boy who followed the two elves.

As they crossed bridge after bridge, passing deeper and deeper into the forest, an invisible village appeared. The dust drifted from tree to tree until finally it settled in one place. Up ahead, Josh could see a big dwelling. This dwelling sat alone, unlike the smaller ones. The small dwellings were clustered together in groups of six and were joined by little walkways from door to door. They had tall cone-shaped roofs, made of straw and reed, which almost reached up to the ceiling of the forest as if to borrow light from the sky above.

The big dwelling was very like them, but much larger than any of the others he had passed. It was magnificent and it sat at the end of a long winding bridge. This bridge was also decorated with carvings of battles and tall posts with riddles, but it also had many arches with faces and names of elves on top of each one.

These must be important elves, like Norlif, thought Josh as he drew closer to the large dwelling at the end of the winding bridge.

There were elves rushing in and out of this dwelling. At least three of them armed with small swords guarded the doorway at all times. As Bortwig approached the door, the guards stepped aside and the door opened. Tigfry turned to Josh.

'You're going in to see Norlif now.' He smiled.

'Follow me, Master Bloom,' instructed Bortwig as he stepped inside.

Josh followed Bortwig along a short, wide hallway. Either side of the hall was lined with elves. They were not staring as the ones outside had, but had their heads bowed.

For the first time since meeting Bortwig, Josh realised how important Bortwig really was. The tree elf, servant of the Great Tree, had returned to his home after such a long

time, and there was respect and gratitude and humility awaiting him. Two more doors opened for the elf and the boy.
They were met by a very old and haggard elf.

'Bortwig,' smiled the old elf fondly. 'You have returned to
us. Feldorn Forest welcomes you.' Then he looked toward
Josh. 'Is this the boy?'

Josh wondered about Norlif's question, and then he
thought back to Tigfry asking Bortwig about him being *The
One*.

Bortwig bowed his head and knelt in front of the old elf.
Josh, not knowing what to do, did as Bortwig did. But before
his knee touched the floor, the old elf stretched out his frail
hand and stopped him; he shook his head and smiled.

Bortwig looked towards Josh.

'It is, my lord.'

Norlif invited them into the centre of the large room,
where they sat on thick fleecy rugs that smelled of fresh pine.
For a moment or two no one said anything. It seemed that
Bortwig would not speak voluntarily, but only if spoken to
by Norlif. Josh, like Bortwig, sat quietly awaiting words.

Finally, Norlif spoke.

'You will be going to see the great wizard?' asked Norlif.

Bortwig nodded toward Josh.

'Em, yes,' stuttered Josh. 'I think so.'

'Wilzorf will be pleased and anxiously awaiting you,'

nodded Norlif. 'He will have wisdom and great news for you. Important things will be said to you and you must be brave, and honourable.'

Josh looked toward Bortwig, but Bortwig's head was bowed.

'What do you mean?' asked Josh.

There was no immediate answer. Norlif just stared. It was a stare of admiration rather than one of judgment.

'Rest your mind now,' said Norlif. 'This is a time for rest and food and peace.' He smiled. 'And festivities! You will travel at dawn to the Wizard. Then no question will be left unanswered. This is the way it is meant to be.'

Norlif leaned over and touched Bortwig on the shoulder.

'Raise your head, loyal servant of the Great Tree. Tonight we are equal. Tonight we will celebrate the arrival of the boy. You have done well, Bortwig, tree elf.'

Norlif pointed towards the far walls of the room and clapped his hands.

Blazing fire midgets rose up and lit the four walls of the room.

Doors swung open from all directions and elves flocked into Norlif's room, filling up the floor and parading high above on balconies.

A huge spit was wheeled into the room and placed beside Norlif.

Josh was starving and his belly ached as the delicious smell hovered toward his nose.

'Now you will eat,' said Norlif. 'Fill your belly so you will be strong tomorrow.'

Large servings were handed to Bortwig and Josh.

'This is really good,' said Josh, devouring huge slices of juicy meat. 'Is it pork?'

Norlif laughed. 'Swine would not enter my realm, let alone pass my lips,' he smiled.

'What is it, then, Bortwig?' whispered Josh as Norlif issued instructions to a line of elves in front of him.

'Wait until you're finished, then I will tell you.'

Josh finished his plate, leaving it sparkling clean. Bortwig sucked upon his fingers.

'Now, don't be startled,' said Bortwig.

Josh didn't like the sound of that.

'It was a glykos,' said Bortwig.

'Like Mirlo?' gasped Josh.

'Yes,' answered Bortwig. 'But not Mirlo. No harm would ever come to Mirlo.'

Josh heaved, but held back, since he didn't want to offend Norlif.

'Don't worry, Master Bloom,' said Bortwig. 'Glykoses are very nutritious creatures. It's all meat at the end of the day.'

Josh was just about to respond to that when music filled

the room. The crowd of tree elves that packed the floor stepped aside.

'Let the festivities begin!' announced Norlif. He clapped his hands and, in the weird way now familiar to Josh, twitched his head with great excitement.

Suddenly, a loud, piercing, screeching noise could be heard outside the room.

Norlif looked at Bortwig and then at Josh. Bortwig jumped to his feet and stood in front of Josh. The doors of the room crashed open and a hideous, fearsome creature thrashed its way across the floor. Josh cringed back in alarm.

'How did this creature escape? Surround it!' shouted Norlif with great authority.

'What *is* that, Bortwig?' Josh shook out.

Norlif answered him, 'A dragolyte! We netted it as it strayed past the forest. Krudon used his evil sorcery to create them from the ashes of the last of the black and red dragons of Mount Erzkrin. They are smaller than dragons, but lethal nonetheless, and as loyal to Krudon as dogs to their masters. Instead of breathing fire, they spit burning bullets of hot rock ash. But not this one! I've had its gut sealed with magical pine gum and its wings snapped. The only weapons it possesses now are its claws, sharp teeth and hatred – great hatred.'

Norlif turned from Josh and slowly walked over to the

creature, watching it as it fixed its evil, damning eyes upon Josh and Josh alone.

The creature opened its jaws. Josh could feel its hatred, hatred so intense that his nose began to bleed.

'Norlif!' called Bortwig.

Norlif turned to see Josh holding his hand to his nose and quickly turned to the creature to divert its evil.

'He sent you, didn't he? And you failed him, didn't you?'

The dragolyte fixed its eyes upon Norlif.

'You've been searching for the boy, tirelessly, and now he is before you, and you cannot carry out your master's evil instructions. Yes! You know you failed him. Krudon would have your hide lowered into the witches' cauldron and mixed with disgusting cankerous syrup for the witches to sip upon.'

The dragolyte raged inside, and returned its evil eyes to Josh.

Josh jumped backwards.

'What's he mean, he was searching for me, Bortwig?' He looked to the elf. 'Why would Krudon send him after me?'

Bortwig was about to speak when suddenly the dragolyte screeched out in agony as it tried to move its wings – its eyes still fixed upon Josh.

Norlif feared for the boy's safety. He looked up to the gathering of elves above him and gestured to one near the edge. The tree elf swung down from the balcony and landed on the creature's back. Great rage and excitement filled the room as elf and dragolyte thrashed across the floor. Every time the evil creature cast its eyes toward Josh, the elves' bows tightened and swords and spears took aim on Norlif's command.

Josh's insight into Bortwig's people had changed. He realised now that they were not just kindly tree elves, but proud and rebellious creatures. They were quite fearless too.

The brave elf was hurt. Blood poured from his chest in the place where the dragolyte had ripped across with its swiping claws.

'Time!' called Norlif, as if boredom was nagging him.

With a powerful leap and a lightning slash, the elf jumped on the dragolyte and severed its head clean from its body. Josh felt light-headed and saw the room start to spin.

Chapter 12

Heckrin's Pass

Josh's sleep was a long, deep one filled with neither dreams nor expectations of what the next day, or even the day after, might bring. As his senses slowly awakened, Josh could feel warmth settling on his face. The rising sun pierced light through his eyelids, revealing intricate flashing patterns.

This was nice, peaceful, non-chaotic – unlike recent happenings. Josh was in no hurry to open his eyes and end his rest. No; he would lie still for just a few more minutes even though he could now hear voices and busy goings-on and fuss around him. But a few minutes were not to be as the warmth quickly left his cheeks and shade once again covered his eyes. A different kind of warmth fell upon him. It wasn't nice warmth like the soothing glow from the sun, but a kind of running, slimy, smelly warmth. It trickled down his forehead and across his eyelids, then came to a gathering on his cheeks.

Josh wanted to open his eyes and jump up, but he felt that fear which sometimes can paralyse a person when he is startled by something as he passes from sleep to consciousness.

Then, it happened again; only, this time, Josh did open his eyes as an even warmer blob of gunk fell into his left ear.

Leaning over a fallen tree and staring down at Josh was a big, fat, ugly, bald creature with a huge trail of disgusting snot hanging from its nostrils.

'Uugh!' yelped Josh. He rolled over to one side just before the gunk dropped to where he had been lying.

The creature smiled at Josh, revealing tiny jagged teeth behind big blue lips.

Josh frantically wiped his face, then tucked his fingers inside his sleeve and vigorously cleaned the inside of his mucus-filled left ear.

'Ah! Awake at last, Master Bloom?' greeted Bortwig, who climbed over the tree from behind the creature.

'What's that?' asked Josh, pointing at the creature.

'Don't be frightened, Master Bloom. This is Baulge. He's a sea ogre, and he's accompanying us on our trip to see Wilzorf. A little protection provided by Norlif.'

'Sea ogre! Shouldn't he be in the sea, then?' asked Josh, observing the gills on the creature's neck.

'Sea, land, makes no difference to Baulge. Very versatile

creatures are sea ogres.'

Josh was standing now. He still felt a bit light-headed.

'Where are we, Bortwig? We're not in the forest. How did we get here?' Josh looked down at the clothes he was wearing. They had been changed.

'And these clothes ... where are my clothes?'

Just as Bortwig was about to answer Baulge moved quickly, thrashing his body to the ground behind the tree. When he stood back up, he was holding a dead hare in his enormous right hand. The ogre looked to Bortwig and held his limp victim up as if to gesture breakfast.

'Excellent, Baulge,' commended Bortwig. 'But I think we will have some fruit instead.'

Bortwig ordered Baulge to eat his breakfast elsewhere as he knew the ogre's savage method of devouring the hare raw would not help Josh's appetite.

He sat Josh back down on the tree trunk and gave him an apple and some grapes left over from Norlif's feast.

'Do you remember the festivities of last night?' asked Bortwig.

Josh nodded.

'Well, I remember the dragolyte and the fight. And I think the elf killed it. Is that right? I don't remember anything after that.'

'Yes, Master Bloom. Artfid, tree elf, did kill Krudon's creature.

But, before he did, Krudon's evil got to you.'

'What do you mean? How?'

'Through the dragolyte's eyes. Its eyes were fixed upon you. It cursed you and damned you to die.'

'My nose bled ...' Josh remembered.

Josh munched on his apple, butt and all, then started on his pear. He had a big appetite and his strength was slowly returning.

'But, my clothes, Bortwig? And how are we here and not back at Feldorn?'

'Norlif's command,' explained the elf. 'As Artfid severed the dragolyte's head clean from its body, blood sprayed your clothing. Norlif believed that this caused weakness to wash over you. A curse in the making. That's why you are in different clothing, Master Bloom. Norlif ordered our immediate departure to the Wizard's domain.'

'But I was asleep.'

Bortwig stood up.

'Baulge carried you. Come, Master Bloom. We must be going. If you are still weak, Baulge will carry you some more.'

Josh joined Bortwig as they searched for Baulge, who had wandered away with his meal.

'I would have liked to have said goodbye to Norlif and Tigfry,' sighed Josh.

Norlif's blessing is with you, Master Bloom. I'm sure your

paths will cross again.'

The elf, the boy and the ogre walked until morning became high sun. The path ended with a cliff edge and a rope bridge, which stretched a long distance over a treacherous drop to another cliff edge. Josh noticed Baulge become twitchy and very nervous as they drew closer to the bridge.

'Bortwig, what's wrong with Baulge?' he whispered.

Bortwig looked over his shoulder at Baulge. The ogre had fallen behind a little and his eyes searched left and right and up and behind.

'Heckrin's Pass,' said Bortwig.

'Excuse me?' asked Josh.

Bortwig pointed ahead toward the bridge they were approaching.

'Do you see the bridge that joins those two cliffs?'

'Yes?'

'That's Heckrin's Pass. Baulge, as hideous and strong as he is, is terrified of Heckrin,' Bortwig explained.

'Who's Heckrin?' interjected Josh.

'Heckrin, Master Bloom, is neither evil nor good; just savage. He is a giant falcon with the hideous head of a crazed, hungry man. He has many jagged teeth and his long, pointed nose can smell warm blood from a hundred miles away.'

'I don't blame Baulge for being afraid of him,' shivered Josh, looking toward the sky. 'He's not here, is he?'

Bortwig shook his head. 'Fear not, Master Bloom. Heckrin hunts on the far-eastern lands of Habilon at high sun.' He laughed. 'Baulge would not be standing here if there was the slightest chance of an encounter with Heckrin.'

'I wouldn't either,' chuckled Josh. 'I'm terrified and I haven't even seen him.'

'Most would fear Heckrin,' nodded Bortwig, 'but Baulge had an especially terrifying encounter with Heckrin when he was just an infant.'

With Baulge close by, Bortwig began to tell Josh about the time Heckrin swooped down from the mist and snatched the infant Baulge from Togilin's shore.

'But Baulge is here and big and well! Heckrin couldn't have eaten him, Bortwig.'

'Heckrin made one mistake,' explained the elf. 'He flew over Feldorn Forest.'

'The archers!' smiled Josh. 'Did they save Baulge?'

Bortwig smiled. 'Yes, Master Bloom! Heckrin still bears the wounds on his left side. It has slowed him a little, but fast, ferocious and ever hungry he still is.'

'So, the tree elves raised Baulge?'

'Baulge fell crashing through the treetops of our forest. As eager as Norlif is to taste different meats, he could not command the slaughter of the infant ogre. And that is why Baulge is loyal to Norlif and Norlif's kind.'

Josh took one look at the bridge and questioned its strength.

'I'm not too sure about crossing that bridge, Bortwig. It looks dodgy.'

Bortwig turned to Baulge.

'Baulge will cross first,' said Bortwig. 'If it holds his weight, then it will hold a hundred elves and at least one brave boy,' he laughed.

Baulge was very nervous. He grunted with dissatisfaction at the situation he was in. Josh walked over to the ogre and patted him on the side; this was as high as he could reach.

'Don't worry, Baulge. You'll be fine. Once we've crossed, we'll be away from this place long before Heckrin shows up.'

Josh looked at Bortwig with a worried frown.

The ogre had not stepped three paces onto the bridge when, suddenly, an infuriating howl came from under the bridge. A very hairy, small creature not much bigger than Bortwig and a little smaller than Josh dragged itself up onto the bridge between the ogre, the boy and the elf.

'Nobody shall cross my bridge!' commanded the creature, pointing its long, hairy finger at Bortwig.

Josh stared at the creature's long black nails with bits of slug guts, bug legs and wings buried deep within.

Yuck! he thought. *Gross!* He heaved.

Baulge leaned over and picked up the creature. It kicked

and raged as it dangled in midair. Bortwig laughed aloud and this infuriated the creature even more.

'Let me down, hideous ogre. Let me down or I shall rip you to shreds and chew on your bones for evening pleasures.'

Bortwig laughed even louder now.

'How dare you laugh, elf. Laugh at a troll, do you?'

Josh was a little confused. *A troll! He doesn't look nasty enough to be a troll.*

'Is he really a troll?' he asked Bortwig, who was now holding his belly as if he had a stitch from laughing too much.

'Let him down, Baulge,' instructed Bortwig. 'No, Master Bloom. Mad Argil is not a troll.'

'I didn't think so,' laughed Josh. He looked at the creature, who was fixing his filthy robe and shaking himself down while grunting up at Baulge.

'Filthy ogre!'

Bortwig walked over to Mad Argil.

'Mad Argil,' said Bortwig. 'If Heckrin knew that you were making claims on his bridge and pretending to be the troll that passed through his gut many years ago, he would send you to the pit of his stomach too.'

'But I *am* a troll!' insisted Mad Argil. 'A *dangerous* troll, too. You shall not cross my bridge.'

Bortwig looked up toward Baulge and winked.

Without hesitation, the ogre rolled his knuckles into a ball and tapped on Mad Argil's head.

Mad Argil fell.

Josh stepped onto the bridge. 'What was that for?'

'For his own good,' smiled Bortwig as Baulge lifted Mad Argil up and flung him over his left shoulder.

'Bonkers Mad Argil may be, but dangerous he is not. Dungers are plenty in numbers and make tasty snacks for Heckrin. Mad Argil is lucky we crossed paths today.'

'So Mad Argil is a dunger. What exactly are dungers?'

'The clue is in the name,' giggled Bortwig. 'Dungers are harmless creatures that forage in dung, usually from trolls or ogres or cyclopses. Big creatures like that always leave something interesting behind them.'

'Uugh! That's gross, Bortwig,' said Josh stepping back a little from Baulge.

'Lead the way, Baulge,' instructed Bortwig. 'I'm pretty sure this bridge will be fine.'

Chapter 13

Flying Terror

Josh held on tight as the bridge swayed from side to side. He dared not look down for it was a long, terrifying distance to the rocky floor below.

'Easy, Baulge,' calmed Bortwig. 'Better to get across slowly than not at all.'

Suddenly, Baulge let out an unmerciful cry. The bridge shook violently as the ogre thrashed about frantically, pointing up at the skies.

'We're going to fall, Bortwig!' screamed Josh. 'What's wrong with him?'

'Baulge!' shouted Bortwig, but the ogre was inconsolable.

Bortwig grabbed hold of Baulge's leg, but Baulge panicked and ran, dragging Bortwig across the bridge. Josh tried to run too, but the bridge was swaying too hard and he was barely able to hold on.

Bortwig let go of Baulge's leg just as they reached the end of the bridge. The ogre danced around with Mad Argil still on his left shoulder. He was in a state of terror.

Bortwig looked back to Josh as the bridge's swaying came to rest.

'Are you alright, Master Bloom?'

Josh quickly got to his feet. His legs and arms were shaking.

He waved to Bortwig, and then slowly began to walk along the bridge again. Bortwig turned to Baulge. The ogre held his head low with shame. He had calmed down a little, but still looked terrified as he pointed to the skies.

Bortwig looked up.

'I can't see anything,' he called, 'but sea ogres are known for their ability to see things that are really far away ...'

Josh could see Bortwig look up to the sky and strain his eyes to see.

'Heckrin!' gasped the elf.

Turning quickly, he shouted toward Josh, who still had a third of the bridge to cross, 'Run, Master Bloom. Run for your life!'

He pointed to the skies. Josh looked up ahead. He too could see something, but it only looked like a dot in the distance.

'Heckrin!' cried Josh, and he began to bolt.

But as Josh approached the far cliffs of Heckrin's Pass, it became apparent that it was not one, but three sets of wings that were flying towards them. It was the witches' cats!

Baulge dropped Mad Argil to the ground, untied his rock club, and took it in hand.

Strangely, the ogre was not as scared now.

'What are they, Bortwig?' gasped Josh, almost out of breath.

'Nasty goblins on the backs of the witches' cats,' answered Bortwig, helping Mad Argil to his feet.

'Witches' cats!' yelped Mad Argil. 'Goblins! Where? I will bash in their heads and throw them over the cliff.'

'Not this again,' huffed Bortwig. 'Quickly! Head for those trees. They might not have spotted us yet.'

The elf, ogre, dunger and boy darted toward the small cluster of whitethorns as the witches' cats grew larger in the sky.

Baulge bravely stepped out from the trees and swung his rock club fast and furiously above his head as the witches' cats swooped down to attack.

Bortwig grabbed hold of Mad Argil, who wanted to help the ogre.

'Quiet, you mad fool!' groaned Bortwig.

Baulge was struggling to keep the cats away. Three were too many. Two of the cats surrounded Baulge while the third flew around the trees and landed on their far side.

The black cat's wings folded and its fangs glistened in the sun's rays. The biggest goblin took a dagger in one hand and jumped off the cat's back. Then he reached into his clothes and took out a whip. He slowly threaded through the trees.

'Baulge!' shouted Bortwig.

Baulge turned his head and as he did, a black cat swiped its massive paw across his head, tearing part of his left ear away. Baulge cried out in rage, then leapt into the air and grabbed the cat's tail as it was ascending. The injured ogre pulled on the cat's tail and dragged it down. The goblin fell off and cracked his head open on a rock.

'He's coming in,' cried Josh as the big goblin drew near the trees.

'Let me go,' protested Mad Argil. 'I will kill him!'

'Shut up, you fool,' said Bortwig. He threw Mad Argil back on the ground behind Josh.

'Stay here, both of you.'

Bortwig approached the goblin.

'Go now, while you still live!' ordered the tree elf.

The goblin grunted, then was distracted by a screech from nearby.

Baulge had smashed the black cat against the ground and ripped one of its wings clean from its body, but the brave ogre could not help the elf as the second cat swooped down to attack him.

The goblin and the elf met eye to eye at the edge of the trees. They circled each other. The goblin swiped the air with his dagger, and then cracked the ground with his whip. The elf made no move beyond silently moving his lips.

Josh looked on in fear. Even though he could not see Baulge through the trees, he knew the ogre was in great combat. He could hear thrashing and screeching and grunting.

Suddenly, the goblin lunged at Bortwig, its dagger pointing toward the elf's chest. Then, it happened. The tree beside Bortwig grabbed hold of the goblin and wrapped its thorny branches around the goblin, squeezing and squeezing until it screeched its last agonising cry.

Bortwig had spoken to the trees, and the trees had listened.

A thought ran through Josh's head, something Bortwig had said to him before, *Mysterious and magical things, trees are, but not talkative!*

Josh smiled. Bortwig had done great.

Baulge swiped at the air, but the black cat and the goblin climbed high out of reach. They hovered way above the ogre, planning their next attack.

Bortwig was heading back into the trees when, suddenly there was a yelp. It came from Mad Argil. He had snuck out through the back of the trees and crept around to the cat that stood on the far side, alone.

The cat walked toward the dead goblin with Mad Argil hanging from its jaws. Josh and Bortwig ran to the opening in the trees, expecting to see Mad Argil's limp body.

'Not fair,' complained Mad Argil. 'Not fair at all.'

He was unharmed. The witch's cat had a hold on his robe.

'Stand back, Master Bloom,' instructed the elf.

Baulge ran over and stood his ground beside Bortwig as the other cat still hovered high. The cat on the ground opened its jaws and let Mad Argil go. Mad Argil complained again and brushed himself off.

Bortwig's eyes enlarged. Mad Argil turned quickly to see the cat's razor-sharp claws raised above his head. It would swipe the dunger's head clean off.

Just as the cat was about to launch its blow, great bravery washed over Josh and he stepped forward to confront the giant cat.

'No, Master Bloom!'

Baulge let a worrying groan.

Josh took his wand from his pocket and pointed it at the cat.

'Leave now or die!' Josh commanded.

'You're dead, boy!' tittered Mad Argil to Josh.

Baulge stepped forward and swung his rock club over his head, bellowing a deep fearsome cry at the cat. But the witches' cat did not back down. It widened its gaping mouth once more and leaned back on its hind legs and began to flap its wings. It was ready to strike.

'Kill it, Baulge!' yelled Bortwig.

Baulge flung his rock club, but the cat lifted into the sky. Baulge had missed.

The witches' cat dived toward Josh.

Suddenly Josh's wand glowed brighter than Josh had ever seen and a blade of fire penetrated the giant cat's chest, sending the creature over the cliff edge.

The last cat screeched, leapt high in the sky and, on the goblin's order, turned and flew away. They were fearful of the great magic that Josh possessed.

Baulge lifted Josh in the air as if to commend the boy's bravery, but Bortwig was in no mood for celebration.

'You could have been killed, Master Bloom.'

Josh was still shaking. Shocked, but overwhelmed that he had defeated the evil witches' cat.

'You can put me down now, Baulge!' he smiled.

Josh walked over to Bortwig and knelt down in front of the elf – face to face.

'It's lucky I've got this,' said Josh, showing the wand to Bortwig.

'Indeed it is, Master Bloom,' sighed Bortwig.

'I need answers, Bortwig' said Josh. 'Why is everything in Habilon trying to kill me?'

Mad Argil jumped to his feet and combed his fingers through his filthy beard, picking out insects that had crawled up from the grass.

'If I wanted to kill you, you'd be dead now. I once killed a cyclops by just staring into its eye. Bet you didn't know that – ha, ha!'

Bortwig looked at Mad Argil with contempt, 'Idiot!' then he returned his eyes to Josh.

'Is it because I'm looking for the general? Is that it, Bortwig? Do they think I have some connection to him, like I'm related to him or something?'

That question made Josh think of home and Henry and Nell and the conversation they had on his birthday about his real parents. Josh was confused now. He sat down beside Bortwig.

Bortwig shook his head. 'We must focus on the path ahead, Master Bloom,' comforted Bortwig. 'And meeting the wizard.'

'But what about the general?' worried Josh. 'I'm supposed to be searching for him, remember – my destiny. I know that's what I'm supposed to be doing.'

Suddenly their conversation was interrupted by yet another yelp from Mad Argil. When they looked to see what was wrong, the dunger could not be seen, yet still they could hear his annoying cries. Baulge was looking over the cliff when he turned quickly and bellowed out tremendous laughter toward Josh and Bortwig.

A blaze of fire shot up into the sky straight up over Baulge's head, followed by another. As the thick smoke cleared, an enormous white dragon appeared. It flapped its wings as it ascended from the cliff's edge, then it landed beside the trees and folded its wings.

A man climbed down from the dragon's back. He had Mad Argil in a neck hold, but Josh could see from his smile and Baulge's delight that he was only playing with the dunger. Mad Argil had been standing with his back to the cliff when he was swiped over the edge.

The man was tall with long dark hair, and he was dressed in full armour. A sword sparkled by his side and bore the sign of a golden arc. He let go of Mad Argil. The dunger marched off into the trees, with disgruntled embarrassment.

'Who's this?' Josh whispered to Bortwig.

Bortwig stepped out of the trees.

'Danthenum!' smiled Bortwig. 'Always makes such a dramatic entrance.'

Mad Argil returned. 'You're very lucky, you caught me by surprise or else I ...'

'Another word from your mouth, dunger, and you will be begging for the tip of my sword to finish you off,' laughed Danthenum.

Then he knelt down and shook the hand of the elf.

Bortwig turned to Josh.

'This, Master Bloom, is Danthenum, knight of the Kingdom of Habilon.'

As Danthenum shook Josh's hand, the white dragon bellowed a loud roar.

'And this,' laughed Bortwig, 'is Smolderin, the white dragon.'

Josh's heart almost skipped a beat when he saw the look on Danthenum's face as Bortwig explained to the knight that he was taking the boy to the wizard Wilzorf. Danthenum turned sharply and looked toward Josh.

'Didn't you tell him?' the knight asked the elf.

'Believe, don't believe,' huffed Bortwig. 'We will travel with or without your help.'

Josh walked closer to them. 'Tell me what, Bortwig?'

Bortwig folded his arms and looked sternly at Danthenum.

Josh turned his eyes away from the elf and repeated the question to the knight.

Danthenum didn't pause or delay.

'The wizard is long dead,' announced the knight.

Josh's face was filled with horror. He looked at Bortwig.

'Bortwig!'

'Don't listen to a word Danthenum speaks, Master Bloom.

The wizard is alive and soon he will be sending for you. Much to discuss, plans to make.'

Danthenum laughed. 'Save his ears from your madness, elf. You know as well as I do that Wilzorf fell at Krudon's evil hand.'

Bortwig looked at Josh and shook his head.

'Very well, then,' said Danthenum. 'I will take you. If you really think the wizard is alive, I will take you.'

Chapter 14

Flight with the White Dragon

Josh watched Danthenum tie three loops in a rope and harness it to Smolderin. Bortwig and Mad Argil quarrelled as to whether Mad Argil should journey back to Feldorn Forest with Baulge or tag along to the wizard Wilzorf's.

Smolderin rested his head in the grass, his big azure eyes fixed upon the skies above, watching to the north. Josh slowly crept over toward Smolderin's head, but carefully kept his distance in case he startled the dragon. Smolderin's eyes rolled and flickered, and his nostrils puffed out hot jets of steam into the air. Josh leapt with fright, falling back into the grass.

Danthenum laughed and then reached out a hand to help

the boy to his feet. Josh was shaken, but tried not to show it in front of Danthenum. He, too, would like to be strong and brave like the knight.

'Don't mind Smolderin,' smiled Danthenum, patting Josh on the shoulder. 'He must like you to even bother to play tricks on you.'

Josh managed a slight grin just to show that it didn't really scare him. Bortwig came over to them, his hands on his head.

'That critter will be the end of me,' complained Bortwig.

'Leave him to fate,' laughed Danthenum. 'You are not responsible for his well-being.'

'Yes, yes, yes,' huffed Bortwig. 'But Norlif and Hink are allies and if Norlif knew that I'd left Argil, mad as he is, to his own demise, there would be bother upon me.'

It was decided. Only Baulge would travel back to Feldorn. He was badly injured, and would only burden the journey to Wilzorf.

Josh was worried about Baulge and whether he would make it back safely, but Bortwig explained to Josh that sea-ogres are very strong creatures.

'Baulge will be just fine, Master Bloom,' he smiled.

On Danthenum's instruction, Josh slipped into the loop on Smolderin's back behind the knight. He was followed by Bortwig, and finally, Mad Argil climbed on the end.

'Are you sure you don't want me to take you to the palace

to see the council?' asked Danthenum.

Bortwig shook his head. 'There is business with the wizard. We must go there first. The council can wait a little longer.'

On those words, Smolderin's wings unfolded.

'Fly to the west,' ordered Danthenum to the dragon. 'To the swamps.'

Josh held on tight to Danthenum's rope as gusts of wind bashed about him. The white dragon released his claws from the ground and with one big push, he ripped high through the sky. The last view Josh had of Heckrin's Pass was that of an ogre belting across the wooden bridge.

There was little to no conversation on the journey to the swamps.

Flying with a dragon was noisy business. Flapping wings and gusting wind muffled out most noises, yet Mad Argil still managed to annoy Bortwig with his outrageous outbursts of screaming and howling. The dunger was having the time of his life. The flight was an opportunity for Smolderin to impress his passengers with his aerial skills through the clear blue skies of Habilon.

At times it was like a roller coaster. All four passengers held on tight as Smolderin nose-dived toward the tips of the pine trees then shifted his giant body to one side and glided through the narrowest of gaps between branches. Every now and then he incinerated large objects that threatened collision.

Josh thought of what his school friends would think if they knew what he was doing at this moment in time.

Imagine! he thought. *I'm actually flying on the back of a dragon. How bizarre is this?*

Josh rubbed his hands along Smolderin's scaly back. It felt like the dragon was wearing an armoured suit. Josh could feel the dragon's heart beating like a roll of thunder, taking long breaks in between each pounding beat.

Still, as exhilarating and mind-blowing as flying with a dragon was, Josh's mind was troubled by Danthenum's words. Was the wizard alive, or had Bortwig led him this far for nothing?

He tried to clear his head of these doubts and enjoy the ride with the dragon. It truly was an amazing experience. More thoughts of home began to run through his head. How was this real? Up to a short time ago, life was normal and uneventful; now he was flying through the air on the back of a dragon.

As Josh admired the wonderful views of Habilon – the snow-capped mountain to the far north, crystal clear streams below surrounded by the greenest of forests – he felt for the first time in his life like he was alive, really alive.

Chapter 15

The Swamps

Josh shivered with cold as Smolderin slowly descended into a thick depression of grey clouds, leaving the blue skies of Habilon a near memory.

Danthenum pointed toward a barren patch of ground at the swamp's edge that was surrounded by a crowd of dead trees.

Smolderin dug his claws into the soft bog. His body sank until the ground oozed up around him, belching and popping poisonous bubbles until he could sink no more.

Danthenum turned to Bortwig. 'Will our wait be a long one?'

Bortwig shook his head. 'Wilzorf will not leave us to the mercy of the swamp,' smiled the elf. His smile was a nervous one. 'Much mischief in this place.'

It was freezing cold in the swamp. Josh could barely feel

his toes, but it was Bortwig's words that sent the coldest shiver through his body. The still of the swamp had an eerie presence and Mad Argil was unusually quiet. This, in a funny kind of way, was disturbing as they had just become used to the dunger's outbursts.

'Are you sure the wizard is alive? I just don't want to wait in this swamp forever,' laughed Danthenum.

Danthenum's humour didn't sit well with the elf.

'He is alive,' argued Bortwig, 'you will see. He will send his envoy.'

Just as Bortwig spoke, Mad Argil broke his silence.

'There!' shouted the crazed dunger, pointing into the blinding mist that haunted the still, murky waters.

Smolderin raised his head, and his eyes widened.

'There's nothing there, you fool,' said Danthenum.

Smolderin opened his nostrils wide and began to inhale.

Josh could feel the dragon's chest expand beneath him.

'Everyone, get off,' instructed Danthenum.

'They're coming to get us!' raved Mad Argil.

Bortwig pushed Mad Argil into the bog. This was to Mad Argil's great satisfaction. He had something to get stuck in; his dunger's instinct switched on. He rolled about and dug his head and arms in deep.

'What is it, Danthenum?' worried Josh.

'I've no idea,' admitted the knight, 'but Smolderin seems

to agree with Mad Argil.'

Danthenum led the boy and the elf around the back of Smolderin, wielding his sword in his hand.

'What about Mad Argil?' asked Josh.

'Leave him,' suggested Bortwig. 'I hope whatever he has seen eats him. He's beginning to really annoy me.' Then Bortwig smiled at Josh.

Suddenly, Mad Argil's head popped up out of the dirt.

'They're here!'

Smolderin exhaled flames of burning terror across the water, clearing the blinding mist.

There were horrifying screams followed by many splashes that rippled tiny waves toward the edge of the swamp.

Then they attacked.

There were hundreds, maybe more. Tiny blue demons no bigger than Josh's hand roared into shore on the backs of slithering swamp eels. They spat a spray of darts into Smolderin's thick, armoured skin.

The dragon bellowed in pain as some of the darts penetrated vulnerable parts of his body, particularly the insides of his ears and under his eyelids. Smolderin's wings flapped violently in rage, and he breathed more fire across the swamp.

The blues were ashore!

Danthenum kicked and swiped at the blues, slashing many tiny heads clean from their bodies, but they were too quick, and too plentiful. Smolderin thrashed the air, swinging around in rage as the blues covered his entire body.

'Run!' ordered Danthenum.

Bortwig turned and twisted, discharging bolts of magical gusts from the palms of his hands and sending the blues tumbling across the boggy floor.

Josh could feel the blues biting into his ankles and climbing up his legs, sticking the tiny darts into his flesh. It was agonising, but he was not going to stop running.

The blues were small and could not match the boy, the elf, or the knight in pace.

Mad Argil was slower than the others. By the time he had reached the thick of the swamp trees, blues were dangling from his long bearded chin, mischievously pulling on his skin, and biting his ears and lips.

The dunger fell.

Josh stopped running and grappled with the clinging terrors, pulling them from his skin. He flung them to the ground, then danced on them, leaving splodges of blue at his feet. Then he turned and walked back towards Mad Argil.

'What are you doing, Master Bloom?' called Bortwig. 'Danthenum!'

The knight and the elf watched anxiously as the boy commanded the blues away from the dunger.

'Leave him!' ordered Josh.

More and more blues gathered but, for some mysterious reason, they did not attack the boy. The blues cleared from Mad Argil, and the angry dunger struggled to his feet. He swiped and grunted at the little swamp terrors.

'Caught me by surprise,' moaned Mad Argil as he limped toward Josh.

'What's happening?' Danthenum asked the elf.

'It's beginning!' answered Bortwig. 'The envoy must be near.'

'What's beginning?' asked Danthenum.

'Shush!' beckoned Bortwig. 'Watch carefully. The boy is becoming brave. Yes! Wilzorf has made contact. Watch carefully! '

Suddenly, the blues scampered in all directions. They screeched and disappeared into the thickness of the swamp. Every single one of them. Even the ones that clung to Smolderin dove from the dragon's back and vanished into the murky waters below. Something had spooked the blues. Something they saw in Josh's eyes when he commanded them away from Mad Argil.

'The wizard Wilzorf has made contact with Josh through his envoy. Magical powers have passed from the Wizard to the boy. The blues sense this, but they sense something else too. The envoy!' said Bortwig to Danthenum.

Bortwig coaxed Mad Argil away from Josh and over to

where Danthenum was standing.

'Now, be quiet,' instructed the elf.

Suddenly something appeared from a tree in front of Josh. He didn't startle or show any surprise; he was clearly already in some kind of hypnotic state.

The creature wrapped her wings around Josh and the boy disappeared inside them. Danthenum drew his sword.

'Wait!' warned Bortwig. 'He is in no danger. It is Eusyphia, the wizard's envoy. I knew she was close when I saw how the blues reacted to Josh.'

Danthenum returned his sword to his side. Eusyphia glanced toward them, and smiled. As she opened her wings wide, holding the sleeping boy against her underside, Bortwig told Danthenum how the witches of Zir had cursed Eusyphia with the hideous body of a giant swamp moth and left her beautiful face unchanged just to remind her of the beauty she once had.

Danthenum recognised this face as Eusyphia smiled to him, then rose up in the air and vanished through the thick camouflage of the trees.

'I remember her!' said Danthenum. 'She was a girl when I was a young boy. She disappeared when bathing in the springs of the waterfalls.'

Bortwig looked to Danthenum.

'The witches' evil has touched many. Come, Danthenum.

We will travel ahead to the palace and address the council. The boy is with the wizard. They must prepare for his coming.'

Chapter 16

The Wizard Wilzorf

Eusyphia gently approached the water, sensitively allowing tiny splashes to spray against Josh's face.

Droplets rolled down the boy's face and kissed his dry, thirsty lips.

He opened his eyes.

He did not know how he had come to be here, or who or what had hold of him, but he was calm. There was no sudden urge to fret or struggle. The beauty of the cascading waters danced in the light of the full moon.

Eusyphia spoke.

Josh knew some sort of insect creature was holding him, but her voice was delicate and filled him with comfort.

'Fear not, boy. Let the magic of the waters wash over you and you will be with the wizard.'

Then she flew into the waterfall. The water did not thrash

against her wings, but gently washed over her with familiarity and fondness. Not one drop of water touched Josh's body as Eusyphia hovered in the thick of the waterfall, then folded her wings and released Josh from her grasp.

'He is on the other side. Go to him.'

Josh walked a few steps, his legs slowly finding their strength.

He turned to Eusyphia only to see her face slowly disappear back into the water. She was beautiful. She smiled to him and nodded. Then she was gone.

As Josh passed through to the other side, the parting waters closed behind him and formed a crystal clear wall of cascading beauty.

Standing small and frail, with his bearded chin bowed before Josh, was the wizard Wilzorf. Josh's heart beat faster. He was happy and relieved that the wizard was alive, just as Bortwig had said.

Pressing his staff against the gritted floor, Wilzorf slowly and awkwardly approached Josh. He humbly took the boy's hand and kissed it. Josh could not believe what was happening.

Why? he thought.

It was as if Wilzorf knew him and had not just met him for the first time. Wilzorf raised his head. The warmest glow covered him and banished the pale, sickly look from his face.

'You have returned, my lord,' spoke the Wizard, weakly but with hope in his voice.

Josh was confused.

These were not the first words he expected to hear from the wizard.

Yes, he had questions, but Bortwig had told him that the wizard would give him answers before he even asked those questions. But Wilzorf's first words to him were mind-boggling, to say the least.

'What do you mean, "returned"?' asked Josh.

'Come, my lord. Come sit with me.'

Wilzorf led Josh over to a large flat stone that sat beside the water's edge. There was a silent moment. It was as if the wizard had waited so long for this moment, and now that it was finally here, he needed just one more moment to prepare himself.

Then, he began to give all the answers that Bortwig had said he would, before the questions were even asked.

'Your destiny,' began Wilzorf, 'has returned you to Habilon.'

'I was here before?' asked Josh. 'But, I thought my destiny was to find the general!'

Wilzorf shook his head with sadness.

'My good friend, General Pennington, has played a part in your being here, but he is not the reason for your journey.'

Wilzorf could see worry filling Josh's eyes. This is not what the boy had expected to hear. It was as if he was now lost in his journey.

Wilzorf took Josh's hand.

'Are you ready to know your destiny?'

Josh nodded. 'Yes, Wilzorf!' he said assertively.

'Twelve years ago, Habilon was ruled by King Borlamon and Queen Trila. And before Borlamon, his father, King Theldor. The king always ruled with his wizard by his side. It was tradition.

'Sygrim was Theldor's wizard. There was a magical bond between king and wizard, symbolised by the magical orb and the king's sword. The King of Habilon entrusted the powers and magic of the orb to his wizard and the wizard would always use its powers for good and good only. This was always the way, until one day …' Wilzorf's head dropped a little.

Josh's eyes fixed on Wilzorf's lips. He hung onto every word the wizard spoke.

Wilzorf continued, 'It was decided that Sygrim would take an apprentice since he became ill. But two, not one, had gained Sygrim's interest. I was one and my brother, Krudon, was the other. For many years Sygrim taught us well and Theldor commended our talents for magic.

'One day, Krudon changed the tradition of Habilon forever. Sygrim had become suspicious of Krudon. His trust in him lessened until finally his fears were realised. Krudon was planning to use the orb for evil instead of good. When Sygrim approached Krudon about it, my brother killed our frail master and fled.'

'Did he take the orb?' Josh interrupted the wizard.

Wilzorf shook his head.

'Krudon knew that the powers of the orb could only be wielded by a wizard who had the king's blessing. Theldor would have driven his sword through Krudon's black heart. So, Krudon fled, knowing deep inside his twisted, evil mind that in time there would be a way to get what he wanted. As the years went by, Theldor ruled without a wizard by his side and the magic of the orb grew dormant.'

'Why?' asked Josh. 'Why did he not trust you? It's not *your* fault that your brother was evil.'

'Thank you, my lord,' smiled the wizard. 'But I cannot question the king's good judgement and he felt that as I was of the same blood line as Krudon, he could not place his trust in me.'

Josh felt a little sorry for Wilzorf as the wizard continued his story.

'Theldor died and was replaced by his heir, Borlamon,' said Wilzorf. 'Borlamon, like his father, was a good king and we became good friends. He promised his dying father that he would not break his wishes and would not return a wizard to his side. Theldor had lost all trust in the wizard's powers with the orb, as he grew paranoid with old age.'

'What happened to Krudon?'

Wilzorf's eyes filled with contempt.

'Krudon hid in exile, practising his evil sorcery until he became more powerful and evil than Sygrim would ever had imagined. He built up alliances with other evils of Habilon, and when he felt the time was right, he attacked the Kingdom of Habilon with merciless fury. Many perished, young and old, and even though the powers of the orb could still be called upon, King Borlamon would not break his promise to Theldor.'

A tear rolled down Wilzorf's face.

'There was nothing I could do. My powers were not enough to save them.'

'Save who?'

'King Borlamon and Queen Trila. They, along with many, died at Krudon's command.'

'Danthenum said that you were killed too?'

Wilzorf shook his head, almost shamefully.

'No! Not true, but that is what many believe. More importantly, Krudon believes it. This is why I have remained in hiding for so many years.'

'What do you mean?'

Hope returned to Wilzorf's face.

'Borlamon had two children. Before the king and queen died, they had been blessed with a baby boy and a baby girl – twins. The boy was first born. He would be next in line, and then his sister if anything should happen to him. Krudon knew this and his next evil plan was to kill them both along with their parents. But they were hidden and escaped Krudon's darkness. Borlamon's dying wish to me was to keep his children safe from Krudon, and when the time was right, return his son, heir to his throne, to power with a wizard by his side. The power of the orb was to be returned to the Kingdom of Habilon. It was decided without hesitation that the general would flee with both babies and take them to the safety of the other world on the far side of the Great Tree, until the time was right for the heir of Habilon to return and rule as king.'

'So Habilon has had no king?'

'Habilon has been governed from the palace by a high council,' said Wilzorf with what sounded like regret in his voice. 'Habilon has always had nobles, but the high council of three was appointed after the death of King Borlamon.'

'You don't approve?' asked Josh. He sensed that Wilzorf didn't agree with the high council.

Wilzorf shrugged his shoulders. 'Approve – don't approve. This is not a judgement for a wizard to make. The high council have had Habilon's best interests in heart just as their king did, but a kingdom needs a king.'

Josh began to wonder about Wilzorf's words; the wizard had said Josh had "returned" to Habilon and told him of how the general had fled to the other side of the Great Tree with a baby boy and girl, King Borlamon's children.

Could I be the king's son? he thought. *Tigfry the elf said that I was 'The One' and everything evil here is trying to kill me. But Wilzorf said a boy and girl. I have no sister. It can't be me!*

Wilzorf continued.

'Before the general made it to safety, Serula, one of the three witches, attacked them. She poisoned Zera, the princess, with a cursed cat's claw. She had aimed for the boy, but the claw only grazed his arm. Zera was in very poor health and it was feared that she would not survive the journey. So she remained behind while the general fled with the prince.'

Josh's eyes widened as he pulled up his sleeve to reveal a scar on his right arm.

'I've had this since I was a baby!' said Josh. 'Well, that's what uncle Henry told me, anyway.'

Wilzorf bowed his head before Josh. 'It is the scar of the cat's claw, my lord.'

'Are you saying that *I'm* King Borlamon's son?'

Wilzorf smiled. 'You are Prince Joshua, heir of Borlamon, my lord.'

'But ... Bortwig?' stuttered Josh. 'Why didn't he tell me

any of this?'

Wilzorf chuckled. 'Bortwig did as he was asked to do, my lord. An adventurous path was to be laid before you, magic and all. The truth, my lord, would have been too great on the other side of the tree. It is tradition in Habilon, my lord that at the coming of age – thirteen to be precise – the heir to the throne must prove both bravery and goodness of heart. As your circumstances were not normal, your test was laid before you in a different, but equally demanding, way.'

Wilzorf smiled at Josh. 'Your sister, my lord, on reaching her thirteenth birthday on the same day as you, also proved both bravery and goodness of heart, just like her brother.'

'My sister!' Josh said out loud. He had never said that before. It sounded and felt good. 'So she's okay, then? She's well, I mean, after the witch's poison – she recovered, Wilzorf. Was she healed by the magical orb? Has it got healing powers?'

Wilzorf nodded. 'The orb, your highness, has great healing powers, but as magical as they are, there are restrictions. A person can only be healed once by the orb, and it cannot bring the dead back from shadow, and a wizard cannot avail of the orb's magic of healing.'

'Like Sygrim, when he became ill,' suggested Josh.

Once again, the wizard nodded his head.

'But what about Zera, Wilzorf? Was she healed by the orb

when she was a baby?'

Wilzorf shook his head. 'Your sister recovered well, my lord, but it was her own inner greatness that healed her and time of course, great time, not the orb. The orb my lord became dormant on the day your father died, and dormant it has remained until recently.'

'Recently?' repeated Josh.

'Yes, my lord. You see, the orb's powers can only be wielded if there is a king or queen to do so, and an heir to the throne of Habilon only comes of age at the age of thirteen. You were only a baby when Zera was poisoned by the witch so the orb's powers could not be used. This is why it was decided that the general hide you in his world beyond the Great Tree and it is also why you have now returned.'

Finally Josh had answers. Maybe not all the answers, as he still wondered where the missing general was. Nonetheless, even though he was happy with the answers that the wizard had given to him, his heart had one question for the wizard.

'What about Henry and Nell, my uncle and aunt?'

'Henry, the general's gardener. Yes,' smiled Wilzorf, 'the general entrusted you to his gardener, then returned beyond the Great Tree to defend the Kingdom of Habilon, the king-dom he had grown to love so much.'

'But he never came back,' added Josh.

'No,' said Wilzorf. 'And so you were raised by the gardener

and his wife, under the watchful eye of the general's daughter. And raised well, as I see before me.'

Josh thought of just how well he had been raised by Henry and Nell. He thought of all the good times they had given him and how they looked out for him and loved him as a son, knowing all along that one day he would have to leave them.

Josh also thought of other things back home – school, his friends, especially Matty, and even the little things, that had once seemed so much a part of his daily life, like the old man who sold newspapers on the corner of Maple Green. All of these things were now so important to Josh.

Have I to leave all of this behind me, forever?

Suddenly everything in front of Josh's eyes began to spin. This was too much for him to handle. *A king!* he thought. *I am a king!*

As if Wilzorf could hear Josh's thoughts, he grasped hold of the boy's arm and led him over to the wall of water.

Josh gazed at his reflection in the water. Was this a king that stood before him?

Wilzorf disappeared for a moment then returned with a scabbard in his hands. He clasped it around Josh's waist.

'Now, my lord,' said Wilzorf. 'You are no longer the boy who set out to find his destiny. Look into the waters and see the king.'

Josh did as the wizard advised.

'Take your wand in your hand and place it into the water. When you return it to your side your true quest will begin.'

Josh took the wand from his belt and holding it tight, he stretched his arm into the water.

The wand glistened in the water's reflection. Then without any warning from the wizard, it cracked a bolt of fire, so bright that Josh had to cover his eyes. Suddenly the wand felt much heavier in Josh's hand.

'You may take your hand from the water,' said Wilzorf.

Josh was no longer holding a wand. He had a sword in his hand. It bore the symbol of an arc, just like Danthenum's, but it also had the symbol of an orb within the arc. It was truly the sword of the King of Habilon.

Bortwig's words ran through Josh's mind.

You will stand before the king and you will know him, and he will know you!

Wilzorf stood before Josh and spoke words of magic.

Sword of Habilon
Sword of Borlamon
Sword of Joshua now become!

The king's sword magically shrank and Josh held it with ease. It was now his sword. He truly felt like a king and not like the scared boy who bravely followed an elf on a journey.

Josh returned the sword to his side and turned to Wilzorf.

'What is my quest, Wilzorf? Can I see Zera?'

'There is urgency, my lord,' advised Wilzorf. 'When the Kingdom of Habilon fell to Krudon, the evil sorcerer took the orb knowing that one day, if he could kill Borlamon's heir, the tradition would be broken and he could wield its powers.'

'But what about my sister, Wilzorf? Can I see her?'

'Krudon has her. She recovered and remained in hiding. Recently, though, not long after her quest of bravery, the Witches of Zir captured her and took her to Krudon's castle. I'm afraid she has once again fallen under the evil spell that Serula cast upon her when she was a baby. She is dying. That is why there is great urgency my lord.'

'I have to save my sister!' said Josh.

'Yes! And you must answer your father's dying wish and return your wizard to your side my lord.'

'Then, we have to go *now!*' Josh tightened his grip on his sword.

Wilzorf held his arm.

'You cannot save her this time without the orb. I fear she will not recover as before.'

'What do you mean?'

'The only way she can be taken from the witches' darkness

is if she is placed beneath the Arc of Habilon. The orb must be returned to its point of origin, where the two sides of the arc meet. Once this is done, the king's wizard can use the orb's sacred powers to save her.'

'Where is the orb? Is it in the castle too?'

'It is not, my lord. It is kept at the top of Mount Erzkrin under the guard of Krudon's dragolytes. Krudon has earned much of his dark sorcery from Mount Erzkrin. If I know my brother, he would believe that the orb's good powers would be weakened and eventually submit to darkness if kept there.'

'Do you think its ability to be used for good is gone?'

Wilzorf's eyes widened. 'I believe not, my lord.'

'Then that is where we must go.'

Eusyphia appeared behind Wilzorf from the darkness of the cave. She held a small sack of food and water.

She towered above the wizard.

'I am too weak at this present time, my lord, to travel with you,' said Wilzorf. 'I'm afraid the dark shadow that Erzkrin has cast over the orb has taken much of my power from me. Eusyphia will take you to Erzkrin. Eat well on your journey and travel swiftly, my lord. Time is not with us.'

'But what about Zera? I will need you to help her.'

'When you speak the words, I will hear them. Then I will answer my king's call. When the time comes, King Joshua, I will be there for you.'

Wilzorf placed his hand upon Josh's shoulder as Eusyphia wrapped her wings around him.

'It is good to be by your side again, my king. Use your sword well. It has your father's spirit within. It will know you and it will not let you down.'

Then, they were gone.

Chapter 17

Krudon's Delight

She lay still and peacefully asleep, yet the witches' poison lurked deep beneath her flawless, pale skin, conjuring its rage to complete its master's evil wish: death! Her gown draped over the table, the ends gnawed away by hungry rats that dared not venture near the princess's cursed flesh.

His black hollow eyes gawked through the sliding door of her dungeon, cursing her beauty as it flickered in the fading candlelight. Krudon had made many visits to the princess's dungeon. It gave him pleasure to see Borlamon's daughter slowly slip into darkness.

Grukh, Krudon's head goblin, came clattering down the treacherous steps, thumping against a wall. Krudon slowly turned his eyes to find the creature checking his hands as he stood before his master.

'What is so urgent that it brings you before me with such

foolish clattering?'

Grukh snorted and grunted, froth gathering at the mouth, dirty rotten teeth behind his devilish smirk.

'A message, master. A message from the witches.'

The goblin held out his hands, revealing a dead bat. Krudon walked over and took the bat from Grukh.

'You've killed it, you imbecile!' he snapped. Then, holding the bat up to his face, Krudon gazed into the dead creature's open eyes, and bellowed laughter from deep below.

'Good news, master?' grunted Grukh, stamping his feet with excitement and content for his master's joy.

'He is coming,' said Krudon.

'He, master?'

'Finally, Borlamon's heir has re-emerged from whatever pitiful stone he has been hiding under.'

'We will kill him, master, and then the princess, and then all heirs to Borlamon will be gone and then you will be almighty!'

'Yes!' delighted Krudon. 'He will come powerless, a weakened pathetic army by his side. The orb is of no value to him, not since Wilzorf is dead. He will not be able to save the princess. Yes, he will come for his sibling, and when he does I will kill him and then the witches can kill the princess as they wish. Once both of Borlamon's heirs are dead, I will crush the Kingdom of Habilon. Twelve long years, Habilon has had neither king nor wizard. They have been ruled by the weak and pathetic council. I could have crushed them if I wanted to, but no, I had to wait for Borlamon's first heir to return. Soon they will feel the wrath of Krudon.'

'And then you will have the power of the orb, master,' grunted Grukh.

Krudon turned away from the goblin and returned his gaze to Zera.

'Finally, I will wield the orb's magical powers and I will command the Zionn Army! Yes, Princess, daughter of Borlamon, heir of Theldor ... finally, I will be almighty and, with the unstoppable fury of the Zionn Army and the powers of the orb, nothing can stop me from spreading my wrath to the world on the far side of the Great Tree!'

Grukh screeched a deafening cry of celebration.

'Go now, Grukh. Gather your army. Prepare them to feast in victory upon the slaughtered carcasses of Joshua's army.' Without turning around, Krudon held out his hand, and the goblin took the bat from it.

Grukh bit the head off the bat, then nodded to his master and scurried away with a sense of urgency.

Chapter 18

High Council

ortwig and Danthenum stood patiently while Mad Argil twitched and scratched and occasionally rummaged through his long filthy beard. The elf was convinced that the white dragon would have eaten the dunger if the two were left alone outside.

The main hall of the palace was very long and very grand. Its walls were decorated with pictures of past kings, wizards, nobles and knights. The end of the hall opened up into a big circle, where Danthenum had knelt momentarily, right in front of statues of Borlamon and Trila.

Danthenum had knelt here many times before, but it was Bortwig and Mad Argil's first time in the palace. The elf and the dunger seemed nervous. Bortwig too knelt, but the dunger just stood and stared.

'Why are we waiting here?' complained Mad Argil.

Danthenum scowled at the dunger. 'Tame your tongue, filthy dunger. The council will summon us when they wish. Don't speak when we are called in.'

Mad Argil grumbled a faint reply, then swiftly sealed his lips on catching a second scowl from Danthenum.

The knight spoke of what to expect once they were called in to see the council, 'There will be three nobles – the one sitting in the centre will be the high noble. This is the one that you should address with the great news of the return of Borlamon's heir, Bortwig, but not before kneeling before all three.'

'I shall tell them to prepare for a great ceremony,' smiled Bortwig. 'Habilon will once again have a king!'

'Not before the fury and evil of Krudon rage upon our kingdom,' warned Danthenum. 'Do not forget, there is great darkness to come before the light of peace can once again shine upon our people.'

Bortwig nodded in agreement with the knight, while once again the dunger grumbled with dissatisfaction of having to keep quiet.

Finally, a small, unremarkable door to the side of the main hall opened and a head peeped around, followed by a hand that waved at them, just a little, to capture their attention. They were ushered through the door and down a long corridor to an oval-shaped room.

The oval room was small. Bortwig had expected more, but Danthenum had told him that this room was once King Borlamon's 'Room of Thought'. It was where he would go alone to reflect on kings of the past and their great victories on the battle fields. In the centre of the room was a single chair, which sat empty beneath the domed rooftop. This is where Borlamon would sit, looking up toward the skies of Habilon. Opposite this chair sat two of the three high nobles of the high council.

Danthenum knelt before them, then nodded a greeting to a fellow knight; the knight was standing in shadow, yet Danthenum knew of his presence. It was to be expected. The High Council was always closely guarded even when there was no apparent threat. Bortwig ordered Mad Argil to stay in the background, well out of sight. Dungers were not a common sight in the palace. The elf then knelt beside Danthenum.

Isbius and Sirg remained still and silent, staring down at the knight and the tree elf. Danthenum knew not to address them. It was not time. The High Council were, at present, incomplete and would not enter any form of debate without the third of their order. Thericus finally entered the room. He slowly shuffled over to his chair, his long, silken gown trailing behind. He sat between Isbius and Sirg, his chair slightly further back and elevated.

'What brings the council to the oval room in the darkest of the night?' Thericus growled down to Danthenum.

Danthenum stood up, and then bowed his head three times, the last bow intended for Thericus.

'My lord, I am accompanied by the tree elf—'

He was sharply interrupted by Sirg, 'We can see that, knight. Answer the question.'

'Yes, my lord, of course. We bring news, my lords. Great news that requires your urgent attention. He has returned, my lords,' smiled the knight.

'Joshua!' said Isbius.

'Yes, my lord! The prince has returned.'

Thericus looked right to Isbius and left to Sirg, then he looked long and hard down at Bortwig who had remained kneeling and silent before them.

'Is this true, Bortwig, tree elf?'

Bortwig raised his head and stood up.

'It is, Lord Thericus.'

'Then, where is he?'

Bortwig and Danthenum spoke together; Danthenum nodded to Bortwig to continue.

'He is with the wizard.'

Sirg began to laugh. Isbius instantly joined him, but Thericus did not laugh at the elf's answer.

'Wilzorf is dead,' laughed Isbius. 'How dare you disgrace

yourself with such foolishness.'

'Quiet!' shouted Thericus. 'You've seen Wilzorf alive?' asked Thericus, his brow rising in anticipation of Bortwig's answer.

'The wizard is alive, Lord Thericus. He is alive and with the prince,' insisted Bortwig.

Thericus continued his questions. 'If the wizard Wilzorf is alive, as you say, then where is he? And, more to the point, where has he been for the past twelve years?'

Bortwig did not like or have any respect for Thericus' interrogations and disbeliefs. He was here to bring great news to the council: Borlamon's heir had returned and with him, so too had hope. The elf stepped forward. The knight in shadow drew his sword, but Thericus raised his hand in disapproval.

'I am not here to entertain Lord Isbius or Lord Sirg. I bring you great news, and you laugh at me!'

'Careful, elf,' frowned Sirg.

Bortwig kept his eyes fixed upon Thericus.

'Twelve long years you have sat in your chairs while Habilon trembled with fear of Krudon and his evils. If Borlamon had not fallen, there would be no High Council. The heir to the throne has returned, Lord Thericus, and you will give up your noble chair and kneel before your king with humility and gratitude for his return.'

'How dare you!' raged Sirg. 'We will have your tongue cut out.'

'Enough, Sirg!' ordered Thericus. 'The council does not need or want Norlif as an enemy.'

Thericus knew that if Bortwig was telling the truth, and Borlamon's heir had returned and the wizard Wilzorf was alive, then he had better show some form of allegiance to his king if he was to remain a noble.

'Do not judge the High Council, tree elf, with such ease, for you have been tucked away in your cosy, safe room in the Great Tree while we have at least tried to pick up the pieces after Krudon took our king and queen from us.'

Bortwig eased his stance. He would at least listen to Thericus' argument.

'The wizard Wilzorf took the king's sword before he disappeared. How are we to trust him, elf? How can we be sure that Wilzorf has not joined forces with his brother?'

Rage came over Bortwig. 'Do not speak of Wilzorf with such contempt, Lord Thericus. He is good and good only!'

'Then why did he take Borlamon's sword?' snarled Sirg.

'The wizard Wilzorf magically changed the sword's appearance and gave it to the general to take beyond the Great Tree and hide, along with Joshua, until the he came of age. The sword is safe and has by now been returned to where it belongs – the hand of our new king.'

'Even if this is true, you must at least understand that it is wise – expected – of the council to doubt the existence of the wizard Wilzorf. If he did not fall at the hand of his evil brother's army, in the great battle, twelve years past, then why has he not returned?'

Bortwig thought first before he would answer.

Danthenum spoke up. 'My lord, I too believed that the wizard was dead, but is it not possible that maybe he remained in hiding until Joshua returned to us? If only to let Krudon believe that he was dead all of these years? If so my lord, would this not prove to the council and the people of Habilon that the wizard Wilzorf is devoted to our king?'

Bortwig nodded to Danthenum with a hint of gratification. Thericus stewed over Danthenum's words, then he turned to Isbius and Sirg, gesturing them closer for quiet discussion, before returning his eyes to the knight and the elf.

'What do you advise, elf?' asked Thericus.

'Your king needs the full support of the council,' answered Bortwig. 'I have no doubt that he will go to Mount Valdosyr to save the princess. But, first, I'm sure he will try and retrieve the orb from the clutches of Krudon's dragolytes on Mount Erzkrin.'

'But our prince is what, thirteen? He is to do all of this and with no upbringing in the ways of Habilon. How is this possible? I worry for his life as I worry for the life of our princess, not long taken from us!' said Thericus.

'I have travelled with our prince, my lord and watched him carefully. He has great bravery — Borlamon's blood rushes through his body, just as it does in Zera,' answered Bortwig with passion.

'I believe our king will meet all adversary with all of Habilon's good and strength in every beat of his brave heart. Will you believe, my lord? This I put to you. Will you believe in your king — our king, the king of all that is good in Habilon?'

Thericus thought again in silence, then whispered to Isbius on his right and the same to Sirg on his left. After more thought, he gestured a hand signal toward the knight.

The knight stepped out of the shadows and stood beside Danthenum.

'You will gather an army and travel to Mount Valdosyr by horse,' instructed Thericus. 'If the elf is right, then your king will need you.'

'Yes, my lord,' nodded the knight before looking toward Danthenum. 'Will you join us?'

Danthenum looked down at Bortwig before answering.

'I will search for him with the elf. His journey to Erzkrin will meet him with many dangers. Even with the wizard by his side, the dragolytes will be a force too great to defeat, I fear.'

Bortwig agreed.

Then, before all agreed it, a howl came from the darkness near the back of the room.

Mad Argil!

'I will march to Valdosyr. No horse required. Just point me in the right direction and I will destroy anything that gets in my way.'

'Who is that?' asked Thericus.

Mad Argil stepped into light, smiling with one hand raised and the other scratching his rear end. Before Thericus had an opportunity to voice his contempt, Bortwig and Danthenum bowed farewell and ushered the dunger out the door.

Thericus turned his attention to the knight.

'Gather your army with no delay. How long before you reach Valdosyr?'

'We should reach the foot of the mountain tomorrow at high sun, my lord. The climb will depend on what evil greets us when we get there.'

'On behalf of the people and our absent king, travel with speed and honour.'

The orders of the High Council rose from their seats and watched as he left the room; an army had to be assembled and horses saddled for the journey to Valdosyr.

Chapter 19

Slygar

Josh had slept through the thick of the darkest hours. As Habilon welcomed another sunrise, he opened his eyes to see the distant summit of Mount Erzkrin up ahead.

'Not too far, my lord,' spoke Eusyphia softly. She held the boy close to her underside firmly and protectively, yet still with a sense of tenderness and affection.

'Habilon is beautiful,' said Josh. 'When I awake from sleep, I expect not to be here, as if it were all a dream.'

Eusyphia, for the first time in their company, allowed herself to laugh, just a little.

'It is very real, my lord, as real as the sun is rising behind that cloud that taints the perfect morning sky.'

'Did you know my parents?' asked Josh.

'I was a child, my lord, when your mother and father fell by the evil hand of Krudon and his army, but I have fond memories of the good in Habilon when they were alive. Our land was always tainted with some form of evil, but your father and his forefathers always protected us.'

Josh felt comfort in Eusyphia's kind words, and he longed to hear more of his heritage.

'Tell me about my sister, Zera? You've met her?'

'I'm afraid I have never had the privilege, my lord, but I have seen her when I have watched in hiding. And I have heard our people tell many great stories of her bravery and beauty and ...' Eusyphia laughed.

'What's so funny?' smiled Josh.

'Forgive me, my lord, but I believe the princess is quite feisty, almost a tomboy, when she is in sword training with royal knights.'

Josh tried to visualise his sister: she was brave, and was trained in sword fighting by royal knights.

I can't wait to meet her! thought Josh. *My sister – I must save her!*

As Eusyphia flew further north, she noticed that, strangely, the cloud was not moving eastwards with the wind.

It was flying south, towards them.

She dipped her head down and descended. She did not want to fly through this black cloud that moved with such conspicuous flight. But it appeared that as she descended, the cloud descended too.

'Hold on tight, my lord. I fear we have trouble heading our way.'

As the cloud grew closer, Josh could hear a faint noise. The noise grew louder and louder. It was a deafening, piercing noise that penetrated the very back of his eardrums. It was almost unbearable.

Eusyphia was flying toward a cloud of bats.

What are bats doing out during daylight? thought Josh.

Eusyphia pointed her head upwards and ascended, but the bats followed her movement. She moved swiftly to her right, then back to her left and dropped her altitude.

There was no avoiding collision. The bats were heading straight for them, no matter what their direction.

'They're heading straight for us!' cried Josh, taking his sword in his right hand.

Eusyphia closed her eyes as the bats screeched toward her, fluttering past her wings, and clattering off the crown of her head. Josh swished and swiped his sword, slicing through wings, but there were too many of them. Then, with a terrifying cry, the bats dispersed on command. Eusyphia quickly opened her eyes. She knew the sound of the terror that ordered the bats away.

Orzena and Serula were flying toward them on their cats. The bats had veiled their attack well.

Eusyphia dove, ducking between the two cats with the

narrowest of margins.

'Get the boy!' screeched Orzena. 'Kill him!'

Choking air rushed through Josh's lungs as Eusyphia pushed herself to fly faster than she ever could have imagined.

It still wasn't enough. The powerful wings of the witches' cats thrashed loudly behind her. She could feel her wings being pulled back as Serula pointed her damning fingers toward her, cursing her with poisonous words.

She spiralled and plummeted toward the ground.

Serula's cat stretched out its daggered paws, trying to grasp Josh from Eusyphia's weak body. However, Eusyphia held on tight to the boy. Every time the cat swiped at him she sent her body into another spin, pulling Josh away from danger, until, finally, her wings regained some strength and she pulled out of the dive, swooping upwards.

But there was Orzena, flying straight toward her. Her cat's jaws wide open, razor-sharp, pointed teeth lunging to strike its fatal blow.

'Turn!' shouted Josh as he pulled his right arm back, his sword glistening in morning sun.

Eusyphia heard her king's command, and with instinctive trust, she twisted her body away to the left. Josh swung his sword across the witch's cat, severing its lower jaw from its head.

Orzena dove from the cat and clung to Eusyphia's legs. She dug her nails in deep, sending agonising bolts of evil shock through Eusyphia's body.

The witch slowly climbed toward Josh.

'You're going to die!' laughed Orzena.

'Cut the leg!' cried Eusyphia.

'What?' Josh couldn't believe what Eusyphia asked him to do.

'Do it now! I have three others.'

Josh looked down, as Orzena plucked her nails from Eusyphia's leg and stretched out her hand.

Without further delay. *SWISH!*

The leg was gone and Orzena with it.

'No!' screeched Serula as she looked down at Orzena's body draped over a tree. Its broken, pointed branch stuck out of her chest.

Eusyphia had blacked out from the shock of her amputation and Josh found himself once again hanging onto her for his life as she fell from the sky. They clattered through trees, which slowed their fall. They crashed through the thick brushwood beneath and landed in a pile of soft leaf-mulch. The mulch camouflaged a large hole in the ground.

As Eusyphia and Josh slid down a tunnel deep beneath the ground, Serula and her cat searched for their bodies. Finally she came across the hole. Serula saw Eusyphia's blood at the entrance of the hole.

'Come!' she beckoned to the cat. 'Take me to Krudon's castle. I will tell him the boy is dead.'

The cat snarled.

'Don't question me! If he is not dead now, he will be soon. There is no escaping Slygar's Pit.'

The cat flapped its wings and Serula screeched with laughter as they disappeared beyond the trees. They headed north-east to bring the good news to Krudon.

❦ ❦ ❦

Josh pulled on Eusyphia's hands, freeing himself from her grasp. She began to regain consciousness as the light from above shone far down to the bottom of the tunnel. Josh knelt over her and tucked his left hand gently behind her head, helping her to sit upright. The blood was no longer pouring from her wound.

'Are you okay?' asked Josh.

Eusyphia smiled. 'Fear not, my lord. Being cursed with the body of a swamp moth has its benefits. I tend to heal very quickly!'

Josh helped her to her feet, as she stood tall on her remaining three legs, her head punctured through a blanket of webs that lined the ceiling of the pit.

'We'll have to try and climb back up, my lord,' suggested Eusyphia.

Josh did not answer Eusyphia. He stepped back from her about three paces, fear masking his face.

Eusyphia slowly turned around to see hundreds of small, spiny, spider-like creatures the size of Josh's hand clinging to the ceiling above her head. They moved along the ceiling, blocking the entrance of the tunnel they had fallen down. The light disappeared. They were in darkness.

'Spinners!' whispered Eusyphia. 'Run, my lord!'

Josh did not hesitate or question Eusyphia's cry. He turned and ran through the darkness.

He could hear a lot of noise from behind him as Eusyphia struggled with the spinners. Then the spinners began to follow him. They scurried along the pit's ceiling, dropping onto his shoulders and crawling all over his body. Josh pulled at them, smashing their spiny warm bodies against the walls. The spinners increased their numbers. They were on the ground and the walls now.

Suddenly Josh could see light ahead. It was coming from three directions and meeting in one point at the centre of the pit up ahead. Josh ran faster, waving his arms and thrashing his body, his hands in a frenzy. As he drew closer, he could smell a terrible stench. He made it to the light.

Strangely, the spinners ceased their chase. They stopped at

the shadowed edges where the tunnel met three more tunnels.

Light shone down from above. Josh was no longer in darkness.

The spinners on the floor quickly crept backwards, into the darkness, leaving Josh all alone. They watched him, hundreds of tiny eyes flickering.

Josh turned around in circles, scratching himself all over and pulling spiny hairs from his itching skin. He looked toward the spinner's tunnel. He thought of Eusyphia and wondered if she was still alive, but he knew that he could not go back to her. He looked at the other three tunnels and then looked to the light above. There was no way out.

Why? Why have the spinners stopped? What are they scared of? he thought while holding his nose to block the sickening smell.

His answer followed quickly.

The spinners turned from the shadowed edges of the pit and scurried away. Josh had heard nothing that could have startled them, but he could feel – sense – that there was something in the pit with him. He slowly turned around clenching his sword. As he turned full circle, he found himself stumbling backwards onto the ground. He held out his sword. The creature's tongue slithered up and down the blade.

Staring down at him, with its large, pink eyes and its long, serrated tongue, was a giant albino serpent. Its long, slimy body

stretched out of one of the tunnels behind. Josh was speech-
less. Even though he tried to use his sword, he found his arms
paralysed with fear and shock. The serpent stretched its tongue
toward Josh. He slid it over the boy's body, then slowly retracted
it back into its mouth.

Then, it spoke.

'I am Slygar,' hissed the serpent. 'What brings a *boy* into my
pit?'

Josh struggled to get any words out. Then he took a deep
breath.

'Accident! It was an accident. Fell ... we fell in.'

'Thought as much,' said Slygar, leaning his head back from
Josh's face. 'And you will want to leave now, won't you?'

Josh wasn't sure whether that was a question or whether
Slygar was teasing him.

'Yes! If you don't mind, that is.'

The serpent smiled, 'Fear not, boy. You would make little
impression on my desires. I will spare your life.'

Josh slowly stood up.

'Where was your journey bringing you when you fell into
my pit?' asked Slygar, noticing the symbols on Josh's sword.

'Erzkrin.'

'Then I will take you. It will be a quicker and shorter journey
underground.'

'You will help me?'

Slygar bowed his head and then raised it again.

'I would help the King of Habilon, my lord.'

Josh noticed something on the top of the serpent's head that reminded him of home — of Henry's story to be exact. He remembered Henry telling him of how the general had left a serpent with a scar on top of his head, when he too fell into the serpent's pit that stank of death ...

Slygar is the serpent in Henry's story! thought Josh. *What am I going to do? He'll kill me for sure. I don't trust him.*

Josh feared to let Slygar know that he doubted the serpent's loyalty, so he had to pretend to trust him.

Josh looked behind. 'There was another. We have to go back for her.'

Slygar shook his head. 'It will be too late.'

Josh wasn't sure what to do. How could he leave Eusyphia behind? Was this the way it was supposed to be? Was this what it was really like being a king, having others sacrifice themselves for your well-being?

Josh looked toward the spinners' dark tunnel once more and then climbed onto Slygar. *There's no going back!* he thought. Then and not for the first time, he thought of the general's wise words in Henry's story — *Forward and fearless — that's the only way to find truth in one's journey.*

Slygar dipped his head and then slowly slid back into the far tunnel, leaving all light and hope for Eusyphia behind.

Chapter 20

A Terrible Trade

Josh clung to Slygar's slimy scales, wondering when or if he would see daylight again. The serpent slithered through the black of the underground for what seemed like a long time.

Finally, light warmed Josh's face once more. Slygar slithered up the walls towards a small opening.

'Keep your head low, King of Habilon,' hissed the serpent as he crashed through the hole with venomous speed, sending stony debris flying through the air.

They were above ground. Josh wiped his eyes as a cloud of dust slowly settled around him. There were small hills on either side of them. These hills stretched across a short distance, then stopped almost at the foot of a large mountain where the terrain radically changed from grass to rock. The summit of this mountain almost touched the clouds above. It was Mount Erzkrin!

'We're here,' announced Josh.

Slygar twisted his head around to him.

'Almost, but not quite. We still have to pass through the valley.' The serpent smiled at Josh, then began to slowly slither toward the foot of Erzkrin.

❦ ❦ ❦

Smolderin flew low to the ground on Danthenum's order. They had been searching for their king all through the night and now they were close to Erzkrin. Danthenum didn't want to be seen just yet by Krudon's dragolytes.

Bortwig was beginning to fear the worst.

Danthenum, on the other hand, was fighting niggling doubts that were haunting his mind. He was beginning to regret addressing the High Council.

'Tell me again, elf,' said Danthenum. 'You're *sure* that the wizard has met with the boy?'

'We've already been through this, Danthenum. Now please keep looking. We must find them.'

Suddenly, Smolderin turned sharply, almost sending the elf and the knight to the ground.

The dragon had seen something.

Smolderin quietly landed at the foot of a small hill.

'What is it, Smolderin?' asked Danthenum.

The dragon lay low, his wings close to the ground, his head resting quietly.

At that moment, they saw. The creatures lurked around the corner of two hills beyond them. Drool dripped from their gaping mouths and fell onto their enormous feet. It then rolled onto the grass and formed big, foul pools. The creatures had been waiting for some time. They looked hungry – very hungry.

'Cyclopses!' gasped Danthenum.

'Valley of the Cyclopses,' whispered Bortwig. 'There is a trade in the making.'

'A trade?'

'Yes!' said Bortwig. 'Look closer, at the one near the back.'

Danthenum could see a cyclops holding two small creatures in each hand, gripping their necks tightly. They wriggled about and made hollow cries from their nostrils.

'They're grildons,' noticed Danthenum.

'Grildons they are,' said Bortwig. 'And of no use to the cyclopses' bellies. Poison flows through their flesh. See how his hands are gloved with cloth and how he holds them away from him? Yes, grildons can kill even a cyclops by just touching its skin.'

'What are they doing with them?' asked Danthenum.

'I don't know,' shrugged Bortwig. 'But cyclopses are loyal to Krudon so we better stay out of sight until they have moved on.'

The elf and the knight sat still, waiting. Neither had any idea of the surprise to come.

They didn't have to wait very long. They watched the biggest cyclops come forward, stepping out from behind the hill.

It slumped across the grassy valley, then turned and gestured toward the one holding the grildons.

Bortwig and Danthenum watched closely. They could see a long tongue slither around a corner, followed by a serpent's head.

'Slygar,' gasped Bortwig. The serpent stopped, only his head to be seen.

'There is going to be a trade,' said Bortwig. 'Slygar must have something for the cyclopses and of course he will take the grildons. Slygar is immune to their poison. His venom dissolves it. He will drag them down into his pit and play with them, chasing them in darkness, before he eats them.'

The elf was right. There was to be a trade – a terrible trade, they would discover as Slygar slithered toward the cyclops, with Josh on his back.

Smolderin bellowed a raging roar and angrily flapped his wings, lunging Danthenum and Bortwig up into the air. Danthenum drew his sword as the white dragon flew toward the centre of the valley, where the trade was taking place.

Slygar quickly twisted full circle. The biggest cyclops grabbed hold of Slygar's tail and pulled the serpent back. He wasn't giving up Josh – his meal – just yet!

The rest of the cyclopses threw axes and rocks at Smolderin, but the dragon dipped and dived, avoiding any injury. Smolderin set a cyclops' head alight, sending the blinded creature screeching to the ground where it thrashed about in desperate torture.

The other cyclopses retreated, fearing the same fate, but the biggest one did not fear the dragon at all; his hunger had driven him to madness. The boy on the serpent's back was his only focus.

In the confusion of the moment, the cyclops holding the grildons tripped and fell onto his back. One of the grildons slipped from his clutches and rolled across his enormous body until it rested upon the cyclops' face. There was a harrowing cry from the cyclops as he threw the grildon from his face and simultaneously released the other one from his hand. The wounded cyclops tore clumps of turf from the ground and its back arched. Blood poured from its eye and the skin on its face swelled, revealing deep, traumatised veins. With a hopeless gasp, it was dead. The grildons scurried away.

Smolderin ascended and turned once more, fixing his eyes upon Slygar this time.

'Get me down low,' ordered Danthenum. The white

dragon dipped his head.

Josh drew his sword and plunged it into Slygar's thick armour of scales, barely penetrating his skin. Slygar lashed his tongue over his head, slapping Josh onto his back. Josh was now dazed. As Slygar thrust his body around in one last attempt to free himself from the cyclops' grasp, Josh fell from him and rolled across the ground.

The cyclops let go of Slygar. The serpent slithered away, disappearing behind a hill. Josh lay on the ground, his sword resting upon the palm of his hand.

'Hurry, Smolderin!' cried Bortwig. The dragon screeched as it approached the cyclops, but he could not breath fire since he was too close to Josh.

The cyclops leaned over to pick up Josh. Smolderin opened his claws. Just as he was about to sink them into the cyclops' back, Josh gripped his sword tightly and plunged it through his captor's heart.

The cyclops cried out. Smolderin plucked the dying creature into the air before he could collapse on Josh, then flung him against a large boulder at the foot of the hill behind the boy. Josh stood up, rubbing his head with one hand and proudly holding the blood-soaked sword in his other.

The prince did well! thought the elf and the knight as Smolderin landed beside the boy. They jumped off and greeted him with fondness and high praise.

Chapter 21

Three Thousand Goblins

F our hundred men and horses had travelled with speed through the night, on into the next day. They finally reached the foot of Mount Valdosyr at high sun. There, Thericus' high knight issued another the instruction to let the army rest. Water was collected from a nearby stream for the horses.

The knights were planning their climb of Valdosyr when a dunger that had trailed on foot disturbed them. Mad Argil popped his head up from behind the rock that the knights were resting upon. His hands were covered in horse dung.

'You won't be able to pass through the mountain that way. You'll have to go further. Yes, further around before you climb.'

One of the knights held his hand to his nose.

'Filthy dunger, take your smell and your madness away from this place now.'

Mad Argil tittered nervously, his madness temporarily on leave. At this moment he was simply a dunger. This was a phase he would go through every once and a while.

'Madness, you say? It is madness to be sitting around plotting and planning right before someone when he is watching you plan your demise?' Mad Argil slowly moved around the knights until he was facing north, straight towards the rocky boulders and cliffs that formed the foot of Valdosyr.

The high knight turned his head toward the mountain, then back to Mad Argil.

'What do you mean, dunger?'

Another knight laughed, 'Tell me you're not going to waste your thoughts on the words of a dunger?'

'Do not laugh so easily,' said the high knight. 'Filthy, smelly creatures they may be, but dungers are known for their sixth sense.'

Just as Mad Argil was about to explain, there was a loud clash up toward the front of the army and screams waved over the line of men and horses until they reached the spot where the knights and the dunger were gathered.

'Told you!' smiled Mad Argil.

'What is it?'

Before Mad Argil could answer, however, it happened again, and they saw it.

'It's as if the mountain has come alive!' cried the other.

'Krags!' yelled Mad Argil.

The high knight gave the order for his men to retreat from the mountain. Then they listened intently to what Mad Argil had to tell them.

'I've heard stories about them, but I've never seen one. At least, not until now,' smiled Mad Argil.

'What are you talking about, dunger?' asked one.

'Didn't you see them?' asked Mad Argil.

'No!' answered the three knights together.

'The creatures at the foot of Valdosyr: krags, they are called. They are what threw the boulders that smashed your men's bones to dust.'

'Servants of Krudon?' asked the high knight.

'Servants of the mountain,' answered Mad Argil. 'Their loyalty is only to the mountain. Anything that climbs the mountain here will be crushed.' Mad Argil pointed to the right. 'That is the path you must take.'

'That will take us too long!'

The high knight agreed with his companion, 'We will try this way first.'

The three knights rode up to the front of the army. The high knight gave the order for the front line to approach the rocks. Thirty men and horses slowly advanced forward.

Mad Argil cautiously stayed near the rear, sanity still somewhat about him. Suddenly, the rocks and stones began to gather and form, tumbling and bashing together, rising up high until they stood enormous and powerful to be seen by all.

The horses kicked their forelegs high and fell backwards as the krags leaned over and picked up the boulders and rocks around them. They flung them with great ease toward their aggressors with merciless rage. The front two lines were smashed to pieces. On a second order, the Habilon army retreated from the foot of the mountain and the wrath of the krags.

Just as the high knight thought he had seen the worst from Valdosyr, his bones trembled and his ears were pulled away from the screaming of his dying men. He redirected his attention toward the north-east, toward the path Mad Argil had advised them to take. From that path came an even greater threat than the krags.

'What will we do, my lord?'

The high knight looked at the other two, then glanced over his army.

'We will stand and fight. Habilon needs loyalty and bravery at this time.'

A knight raised his right arm and addressed the army with

a roar.

'For Habilon!'

The high knight turned to him. 'Go, travel with speed.' Then he looked toward Mad Argil. 'Bring the dunger with you. He has no purpose here.' The high knight looked to the other one last time. 'Go to the palace and warn the council. They must flee Habilon. GO NOW!'

Then the knight faced north-east again. His eyes fixed upon the three thousand armed goblins marching toward them.

Chapter 22

The Orb

Smolderin rested low on the western edge of Mount Erzkrin, well out of sight from anything watching from high above on the summit.

Josh, Bortwig and Danthenum had been climbing for a short while, and Josh had been telling the elf and the knight of his meeting with the wizard, when, unexpectedly, there were explosions from the mountain's summit. Hot molten rocks had blasted up into the twilight skies of Habilon; Krudon's dragolytes were making their presence felt!

'Quickly!' ushered Bortwig. 'The orb!'

Josh and Danthenum grasped onto the rocks and followed Bortwig up to the top of Erzkrin's western edge. It was the highest point of the mountain.

They peered through a gap in two large rocks, glaring down at the lower edges of Erzkrin's summit. Dragolytes, red and black, lined the entire edge. There were more red dragolytes than black; the red ones were the most fearsome, but black dragolytes were cunning, tactful and very useful in combat.

'They're not keeping watch,' noticed Danthenum. 'It looks like they are waiting for something to happen.'

Suddenly, Danthenum's words were confirmed. Krudon walked out from under a ledge, stopped and raised his right hand.

'The orb!' gasped Bortwig.

The orb had been kept hidden in a cave in Erzkrin's summit, guarded by the dragolytes, ever since the day Krudon took it from its royal stand in the southern tower of the king's palace.

'Now what do we do?' worried Josh. He was frightened now. He had shown great bravery on his journey, but a part of him from his old world – his life with Henry and Nell, with his school friends, in his familiar safe surroundings – was still with him, in his heart, reminding him of how dangerous the land of Habilon was.

'Listen,' beckoned Danthenum.

Krudon began to speak to his dragolytes.

'Evil of Habilon, our time has come.'

The dragolytes flapped their wings in celebration and leaned their heads back, spitting molten rocks high into the sky. Krudon bellowed with laughter, silencing the celebrations.

'Finally, Joshua, Borlamon's heir, is dead.'

Once again, the dragolytes celebrated, screeching deafening cries.

Josh looked at Bortwig, then Danthenum. Danthenum shook his head.

Bortwig smiled. 'He thinks you're dead. This is good.'

'Good?' said Danthenum. 'Krudon has the orb. How is this good?'

'We have the element of surprise,' smiled the elf. 'Worry not for the orb. We will just have to get it back.'

Josh's face creased up with worry, 'Zera!' he gasped. 'If Krudon thinks I am dead then he'll kill Zera!'

Krudon turned full circle, holding the orb up high. The three onlookers dipped their heads as Krudon's eyes passed over their hiding place. Then, once again, his back was turned to them.

Krudon spoke his final words from the summit.

'Fly now, creatures of Erzkrin. Fly south to the arc. Soon the orb will pass over from good to evil and we will crush anything that stands against us!'

One by one, the dragolytes rose into the air and headed south, as Krudon had commanded. Krudon turned around and walked away from the ledge's edge. Two dragolytes, one black and one red, met him. They were attached to a chariot. Krudon stepped onto the chariot. Josh, Bortwig and

Danthenum ducked for cover as the chariot swooped up into the sky and flew over their heads, heading south.

'Come,' ushered Bortwig. 'We must go to Valdosyr and save the princess.'

'But the orb,' worried Josh. 'We need the orb to cure her.'

'Our quest has not changed, my lord,' said Bortwig, raising his hand to Josh's shoulder.

'We must still free Zera from Krudon's castle. Worry not for the orb. Krudon will soon realise you are not dead when he places the orb into the arc and it rejects his evil hand.' The elf smiled, but deep down, he worried if the orb had been in Erzkrin's dark shadows for too long.

Bortwig grabbed Josh's arm as they descended Erzkrin, 'Wait!'

Danthenum drew his sword. 'What is it, tree elf?'

'I can smell it,' warned Bortwig.

'Smell what?' asked Josh.

'Quickly,' warned Bortwig. 'We must get to Smolderin.'

They began to shuffle down the rocky edge, their feet slipping along the loose, blackened stones of Erzkrin.

They did not sense that something was watching them from above – it was a black one, a smart one, and as the others flew south, it crept out of sight and around the northern edge of Erzkrin. Suddenly, Bortwig fell to his feet and cried out in agony. A burning lump of rock ash had lanced his left arm, leaving a deep, singeing wound. Then the dragolyte screeched.

Danthenum turned quickly, swiping his sword through the air as Krudon's creature swooped in to attack. He missed! Josh helped Bortwig back to his feet. The elf was in a lot of pain, but it was not a fatal blow.

The dragolyte stopped in mid-air, flapping its long, scaled wings. It fixed its fiery eyes upon one thing and one thing only: the boy. Josh wielded his sword with both hands, pointing it at the creature.

Danthenum stood in front of Josh, 'Stand down, my lord.'

Josh and Bortwig leaned back into the mountain as the knight stepped up onto a large rock, positioning himself between the creature and his king.

Danthenum curved his right arm, pointing the sword at the dragolyte. With his left hand he beckoned the creature to him. The dragolyte screeched, and then flapped its wings in a rage. It attacked, spitting rock ash at Danthenum, but the knight slashed the onslaught of burning rocks into pieces with noble skill.

The dragolyte opened its enormous mouth, its tongue draping over tracks of curved, jagged teeth. It opened its claws as it plunged toward Danthenum.

Suddenly, a bellowing roar rippled across Erzkrin's western edge as the white dragon raged toward the dragolyte.

The dragolyte twisted its head full circle to see Smolderin flying toward it. Just as the evil creature pulled out of its attack to flee Smolderin, Danthenum lanced the tip of his sword across its belly, spilling its insides.

Josh pulled Bortwig to one side and Danthenum jumped to his feet as the dragolyte crashed into the mountain. The creature lay still and gasped out a few long breaths of air. As Smolderin clung onto the side of Erzkrin, Josh helped Bortwig onto the white dragon's back. Danthenum stood above the black dragolyte and plunged his sword through the creature's heart.

It was time to leave Erzkrin and its evil behind.

Chapter 23

Valdosyr

Smolderin descended toward the stream on Danthenum's order. Bortwig needed water and his wound needed to be cleaned.

As the white dragon flew low, Habilon's moon crept out from behind the shade. Its light shone across the water, revealing the carnage of bodies in the surrounding area.

'Over there, Smolderin,' called Danthenum, pointing down to something moving along the grass.

It was the high knight; he was badly injured. His lower right leg had been crushed and a large dagger dug deeply into his back. He raised his head to Danthenum, his face ghastly and his skin darkened with dirt.

'Danthenum!' he gasped, grasping his arm.

'Easy Melchard,' comforted Danthenum. He knew it was only a matter of time before his spirit passed over.

Melchard needed to speak.

'Goblins,' gasped the dying knight.

Josh had been tending to Bortwig's wound when he came over and knelt beside Melchard. Melchard slid his shaking arm across Danthenum, reaching for Josh. Josh reached out and held his hand. Tears ran from Melchard's eyes, cleansing the dirt from his face. He smiled.

'Joshua!' he gasped.

Josh's eyes were teary. He nodded.

'My king!' said Melchard with ease. His struggle was nearing its end.

He turned his head sharply to Danthenum.

'The people have been warned ... goblins ... three thousand ...' Melchard's eyes rolled and his voice grew frail as he squeezed Josh's hand.

'Message sent ... the people ... goblins ...' he said before he drew his last breath.

There was nothing waiting for them as they approached Krudon's castle: no goblins, no dragolytes; nothing at all.

Krudon had left his castle empty and unguarded. The princess' captivity was over. In Krudon's mind Borlamon's heirs were dead, so he was now busy directing all of his evil toward the arc.

Cyclopses and blues moved from the west. Even krags left their mountain to join Krudon's goblin army from the east and march south.

Bortwig could never have truly imagined the fury that gathered south as he helped Josh search for Zera in Krudon's dungeons. But that was a worry for a later time. Finding Zera was the quest for now.

As Danthenum led them through the damp, darkened corridors, Josh and Bortwig wondered if they would find the general. But their hopes were shattered. There was no trace of the general anywhere. Finally, they found the steps that led them to the princess' dungeon. To their shock and disappointment all that rested near the table where the princess had slept were gnawed pieces of her robe on the floor.

'She's gone!' cried Josh. 'Where is she? Bortwig, what has he done with her?'

Bortwig, like Danthenum, stood in front of the table, mesmerised.

They had no answer.

Suddenly, they heard something scurrying down the steps. Danthenum and Josh drew their swords. A shadow appeared down the last few steps, before the figure followed. It was Wilzorf!

Bortwig's eyes lit up. 'Wilzorf!' gasped the elf with relief.

Wilzorf entered the room. He appeared to be in great health.

The wizard explained to them how he had travelled with speed, matched by no other. He had travelled with Heckrin, who had been hunting to the west when he came across an injured creature climbing out of Slygar's pit. Eusyphia! Heckrin remembered the gentle way she had found him in the swamps and had cared for the wounds he suffered from the archers. In return, on Eusyphia's request, he brought her to the waterfalls, where Wilzorf looked after her.

'Is she okay?' worried Josh.

'She is well, my lord,' smiled Wilzorf.

Wilzorf went on to explain how he saw the dragolytes fly south from Erzkrin and knew that the orb had been taken from Erzkrin's dark grasp.

'It was then that strength returned to me,' said Wilzorf. 'My powers quickly returned to me, as if the shadow of Erzkrin had been lifted.'

'Krudon has the orb!' cried Josh.

'Yes, my lord, I know,' answered Wilzorf. 'I have seen his evil moving south. Habilon is destroyed and now Krudon and his evil armies move towards the arc.'

Josh turned toward Zera's table.

'She's *gone*, Wilzorf. What has he done with her? Is she dead?'

'Come,' Wilzorf shook his head. With that, the wizard led them out of the dungeons.

Wilzorf quickly ushered the others to the eastern wall of Krudon's castle, where Heckrin was sitting on a pier and cruelly playing with a rat.

'There!' said Wilzorf, pointing down toward the cliff below the wall.

'What is it, Wilzorf?' asked Bortwig.

'It is the princess's necklace,' said Danthenum.

'The witch, Serula, has taken her,' said Wilzorf.

'Where?' asked Josh. 'How do you know for sure?'

Wilzorf ran his staff along the wall. Froth and small black hairs gathered upon it.

'From her cat,' informed Wilzorf.

'Lisagor!' said Bortwig.

Wilzorf nodded.

Wilzorf and Bortwig knew what Serula's plans were for Zera.

They explained to Josh and Danthenum how Serula would offer Zera's spirit to the shadows of Lisagor.

'The fields of Lisagor are evil,' said Wilzorf. 'They are where all evil spirits end up when light is taken from them.'

'The shadows come out every sunrise and search the land for evil spirits that linger around their dead bodies. Then they take these spirits to Lisagor and drag them deep under the dirt where they are damned forever,' added Bortwig.

'But what does the witch have to gain from taking Zera there?' asked Danthenum. 'She's not evil.'

Wilzorf explained how the good light comes for those

with good spirits before the shadows of Lisagor can get to them.

'But the shadows will take any spirit they can and sometimes they do get to good spirits first. These captive good spirits, then, in time, turn into greys: harmless shadows that linger around Lisagor's fields and never go underground.

'The good light will not enter Lisagor,' explained Wilzorf. 'If Serula kills Zera in Lisagor at the break of dawn, the shadows will take her. The spirit of a princess would be of high interest to the shadows of Lisagor, and, more than likely, Serula would be granted the return of her two sisters, Orzena and Urtilia, for this offering.'

Josh looked to Bortwig.

'I've seen the shadows,' he cried. 'In the Great Tree.'

Bortwig nodded.

'Then you know what danger lies ahead for Zera,' said Wilzorf. 'We must go, quickly, before the sun rises. I fear it will be too late for our princess at that time.'

'We must go now,' added Bortwig.

'You, my good friend,' said Wilzorf, 'will travel to Feldorn with the white dragon and the knight. Much help is needed there.'

Bortwig looked a little disappointed.

As Heckrin lifted from the pier with Wilzorf and Josh, Wilzorf smiled and nodded toward the elf, but deep worry hid behind the wizard's smile.

'There will be great battles before the next sunset. The orb will decide Habilon's fate. I hope, my good friend, we will meet in victory at the Arc of Habilon.'

Bortwig and Danthenum sat upon Smolderin and waved as Wilzorf and Josh flew south with Heckrin toward the damning fields of Lisagor.

Chapter 24

Lisagor

Heckrin would not fly any further as he believed that the living had no place in Lisagor. He sat still, camouflaged among the branches of the trees, watching Wilzorf and Josh wade through Lisagor's long grasses. The darkness was still deep, but Wilzorf feared dawn would shortly break the night's reign and that it would be too late for the princess.

Even with his powers almost fully restored, Wilzorf knew that he would not be able to defeat the shadows. Yet he would not have taken his king into the evil plains of Lisagor if the Great Tree had not shown the shadows to him at the time of his passing between the two worlds.

'What are we looking for?' asked Josh as they walked further and further across the plains of Lisagor. 'Where will Serula have taken Zera?'

'I don't know, my lord,' answered Wilzorf. 'I fear the witch is lying low, waiting for sunrise. There is no great doorway to the underworld. Lisagor has no magnificent monuments standing glorious and proud; it just has fields of dirt that cover the great darkness beneath. The shadows will come up, my lord, and they will change the landscape of Lisagor as they dance among the grasses in the morning light.'

'Look, Wilzorf!' cried Josh.

Peering over the far horizon of Habilon, the sun's first light began to emerge.

'We must hurry, my lord,' warned Wilzorf as he broke into a run.

Suddenly, Josh could see a light shadow running alongside him. It was not a black shadow, but a grey.

Then, another ran beside Wilzorf. The shadows reached out their hands to them. Wilzorf nodded to Josh and they grasped the shadows' hands. They were whizzed into the air and sped across Lisagor's fields as light began to fill the sky. The darkness receded.

Up ahead, they could see the witch, Serula, dancing around Zera, who was lying across a large rock. Serula was chanting evil poison from her lips. Grasped between her two hands was a long, pointed dagger. She was about to kill the princess.

For the first time since Josh had stepped beyond the cherry tree, great hatred rushed through his veins. He had no memory of his sister, but she was his sibling – his twin – and Josh could almost feel the witch's dagger pierce his own heart as she waved it in time with her evil chant, preparing to add one of the final pieces in Krudon's dark, malign jigsaw.

Black shadows emerged from the ground and rose up high above the ritual. Like the witch, the shadows danced around in circles until they formed into one big, black shadow that enveloped the witch and the princess in darkness. Wilzorf reached out his staff in a desperate attempt to stop the witch. But was he too late?

❧ ❧ ❧

Krudon's armies had surrounded Feldorn.

They were attacking from the north, west and east, and even from the south, boldly in front of Habilon's Arc. Krudon's time had come. The evil sorcerer had waited so long for this moment. His chariot hovered in midair next to the orb's intended resting place, where the two sides of the arc met.

He took the orb in hand and leaned into the arc, looking down toward Sorkrin.

'You will bow before me, great warrior, and I will take your army to the other world. We will be unstoppable!' he cackled.

Then he placed the orb into the arc.

Suddenly, a blinding beam of white light shot out of the arc and headed for Lisagor. Wilzorf and Josh could hear Krudon's agonising screams across the land.

'The orb has rejected Krudon,' gasped Wilzorf. He looked over at Josh. 'It is reaching out for its king ...'

'Wilzorf!' cried Josh, pointing ahead.

Serula was standing over Zera, her arms raised above her head.

The evil witch lowered the dagger toward the princess's chest.

Suddenly, the light of the orb entered Lisagor.

'No!' cried Wilzorf. He threw his staff into the path of the light as it swiftly moved across Lisagor's fields.

Just as Serula's dagger touched the princess's robe, the orb's light shot Wilzorf's staff through her chest. The force of the blow sent the witch and the dagger crashing to the ground.

Light refracted from the staff up into the mass of black shadow, shielding the princess from Lisagor's evil. Then, they appeared: not one, not two, but dozens of grey shadows danced all around the princess until one of them lifted her from the rock and swept her away toward Wilzorf and Josh.

As Wilzorf's shadow turned around, the wizard leaned back and reached out for his staff. The staff shot out of Serula's chest and flew back into the wizard's hand. Suddenly, the orb's light disappeared.

The black shadow furiously separated into hundreds of smaller shadows.

The greys scattered as the black shadows chased across the fields after the wizard, the king and the princess. The three grey shadows dipped and swirled, avoiding the evil grasps of the others, but the black shadows were closing in and still the greys had not reached the edges of Lisagor.

Suddenly, Wilzorf could see Heckrin flying toward them. The creature had abandoned his fears and come for them! Some of the black shadows broke away from the others and flew toward Heckrin, but Heckrin was too fast even for the shadows.

As Heckrin swooped under the greys, they let go and the wizard, Josh, and the princess fell onto Heckrin's back. Wilzorf held on tightly to the sleeping princess as Heckrin swept them away from the evil of Lisagor. The creature headed swiftly south on Wilzorf's command. They flew in the direction of Togilin's shore. This was the quickest way to the Arc of Habilon.

Josh gazed at his sickly sister. He, too, wrapped his arm around her waist, in an effort to protect her. It was as if he was telling her that he had returned and he would be strong for her, for both of them. His thoughts raced as they flew towards the place where his journey in Habilon, began.

He thought of how Zera and he looked alike. Even though she looked poorly, there were recognisable similarities; they had the same nose, and their hair was identical in colour. Josh then thought of his parents, his real father and mother, Borlamon and Trila, trying to force long-lost memories of them to the front of his mind.

Then he thought of Henry and Nell and how he always thought of them as his closest loved ones. His mind was alive with thoughts and this fuelled a fire in his heart — a fire that would never burn out. Bravery once again washed over him.

I am the King of Habilon! he thought as Heckrin carefully descended from the clouds.

Chapter 25

The Final Battle

Feldorn was a battlefield! Norlif had opened his kingdom to those who had escaped Habilon's ruin, and now Krudon's evil was inflicting their wrath on Feldorn. Cyclopses and krags thrashed through Feldorn's trees and sent Norlif's tree elves to the floor of the forest, where they were picked off one by one by the blues that hid beneath the thick foliage.

Danthenum and Smolderin were in aerial combat with dragolytes. Smolderin took out two, maybe three dragolytes with each raging breath of fire.

Feldorn's archers bombarded the southern grasses between the forests and the arc while a small army of Habilon's men and Norlif's warrior elves, along with one thousand of Hink's dungers, struggled against Krudon's fierce and merciless goblin army.

There was no trace of Bortwig.

As Heckrin flew over Togilin's shore, Josh could see a colony of sea ogres swimming away and leaving the deserted beaches behind. This was not a good sign, according to Wilzorf. The sea ogres feared the worst and were leaving Habilon's troubled land.

As they neared the arc the cries of battle rattled their ears. The torched skies above Feldorn sent shivering fear through Josh's body.

As they flew over the arc, they could see the bodies of Krudon's dragolytes. The red one was still attached to the chariot, but its head dangled from its neck in the spot where the orb must have lanced it. The black dragolyte was further away, lying beside the hand of Sorkrin that rested upon the ground.

On Wilzorf's command, Heckrin circled the arc twice before landing on the grass beneath it. There was no threat left! It appeared that evil and good had finished their contest in this sacred place and all that was left was death.

As Wilzorf laid the princess beneath the arc he could see Krudon's mutilated body leaning against the wall to the side of the arc. In addition to his right hand being singed off, the evil sorcerer had deep, smouldering burns all over his body and face. Although the orb had shown him little mercy, he was not dead. His breaths were hampered and distant.

Wilzorf stood in front of Josh, and then knelt before him.

'My king, is it your wish to return the good of the orb to your wizard?'

Josh placed his hand upon Wilzorf's shoulder.

'It is my wish.'

Suddenly, the orb began to glow.

Wilzorf stood up, and then looked up to the orb.

The wizard raised his staff toward the top of the arc.

The light from the orb grew brighter and brighter until it reached out to Wilzorf's staff.

'Great Orb,' began the wizard, 'symbol of all that is good in Habilon.' Wilzorf reached out his left arm toward Zera. 'Banish all darkness and evil from the princess and return her to us.'

The light shot through Wilzorf's body and out through his arm and into Zera until it returned to the orb, forming a triangular beam.

With a sudden flash in the sky, the light vanished and Wilzorf fell to his knees.

Josh ran over to the wizard and helped him to his feet.

'Look, my lord,' gasped Wilzorf.

Zera was standing beneath the arc, dazed, rubbing her hand across her forehead. For the first time in twelve years brother and sister, Borlamon's heirs, were reunited. Josh ran over to join his sister beneath the arc. Zera instantly knew him. She had been told about her brother, the prince who lived on the far side of the Great Tree, by the knights who had trained her. Brother and sister just stared at each other with disbelief, until Zera broke their silence and cried out to her brother with the faintest of cries.

'Joshua!'

The twins embraced and felt each others' hearts beat together for the first time since they were infants.

As Zera joyfully hugged her brother, Bortwig ran up the steps in front of the arc. The elf had sneaked pass the goblin army with Mirlo's help.

Wilzorf smiled at Bortwig, happy to be standing with him beneath the arc, but victory was not yet with the good of Habilon.

'We must act quickly, my lord,' beckoned Wilzorf, pointing toward the fields beyond.

Krudon's goblins were advancing toward the arc. As Wilzorf and Josh ran toward Sorkrin, Krudon opened his eyes and bellowed out laughter.

'Kill him!'

Suddenly, the black dragolyte lifted its head and screeched out. It had been playing dead. The evil creature rolled its head around to them, spitting a barrage of molten rocks.

Wilzorf shielded Josh from the onslaught with his staff. He cast bolts of fire back at the dragolyte as it leapt up into the air and sent it tumbling to the ground. He pointed his staff toward the orb. As the orb cast a ray of light toward the wizard, the dragolyte spat one last rock ash at Josh. Wilzorf caught the orb's light and thrusted it straight through the dragolyte, killing the evil creature instantly. But he had no time to save Josh. As the molten bullet sped toward Josh's chest, the boy felt himself being pushed aside to the ground. The dragolyte's evil hit Bortwig in the chest as he leapt through the air to save his king.

Josh crawled over to Bortwig and held the elf as he whimpered and shivered. He was so cold! Zera knelt beside him and placed her warm hand under his head.

Wilzorf glared over at Krudon. The sorcerer was laughing.

'Cry not for the elf,' said Krudon. 'He is but a pointless creature. Save your tears, boy, for when you stand before your parents' tombs and know that you will never know them. *I* took that from you!'

Josh turned his head with hatred in his eyes. He lifted his sword and pointed it at the sorcerer.

Krudon spluttered blood from his mouth. Death was near.

He looked toward Wilzorf. 'I am dying, brother, but I will not die alone. Do you remember when Sygrim taught us of a magic known as *abreptus anima*?'

Wilzorf stared at Krudon in horror.

'I remember well! *Abreptus anima*, an ancient magic of Habilonian wizards that was used to capture – entrap – the body and soul of a person, hiding it within the wizard's body so it could be used to see things and places and people connected with the entrapped!'

Krudon once again coughed blood.

The evil sorcerer looked toward Josh, 'Don't be afraid to grasp your destiny boy!' he laughed.

At first Josh thought that the dying sorcerer was going mad in his last breaths, but then he remembered those words — the general's words — in the library. The painting on the wall in the library spoke those words to him and when he told Bortwig, the elf had thought it was strange and part of the dark changes in the manor ...

'The general!' cried Josh.

Realising that his evil brother was drawing his last breath, Wilzorf knew that there was only one way to break the sorcerer's spell; he ran over to Krudon and drove his staff through his chest.

Suddenly, the roars of goblins could be heard approaching the steps of the arc. Josh looked to Wilzorf and the wizard nodded toward Sorkrin. Josh ran to Sorkrin and dove across the grass, reaching out his hand.

As goblins ran up the arc's steps, Wilzorf met them with fury from his staff, while Zera stood bravely shielding Bortwig with a dagger she had taken from the fallen elf.

Josh rested his sword upon Sorkrin's right hand.

'Your king needs you,' he announced. Light from the arc beamed down on Sorkrin and his army – the Zionn Army awoke.

Sorkrin looked upon his king and then commanded his army forth. A long trail of giant stone warriors followed Sorkrin as he thrashed his way through the goblin army, clearing the arc and the fields it looked upon of all evil. Zera called out to Josh and Wilzorf as they watched victory near.

The wizard and his king could not believe what they saw before them. Krudon had spoken the truth: General Edgar Pennington stood up from Krudon's dead body and walked a few steps away from it, stopping then turning around and looking back.

Josh watched as Wilzorf walked over to the general and stretched out his arms to embrace him.

'My good friend,' smiled the wizard. 'You have returned to us.'

The general smiled back at Wilzorf. 'Tell me, wizard,' he said in a weakened voice. 'Has victory crossed to our side? I would like to go home if it has.'

Wilzorf nodded. 'Habilon has a king once more.' He looked toward Josh.

The general reached out his hand to King Joshua. 'You have grown, boy. I shall praise Henry on my return.' Pain rushed through his body. The spell had put great strain on the general's old body.

Wilzorf looked around to the Great Tree.

'The flowers are almost gone,' said the wizard. 'General, you must go now.'

Darkness followed the fourth sunset since Josh set out on his journey. Just as Bortwig had foretold, Thericus knelt before his king and Sirg placed the crown upon Josh's head, while Princess Zera smiled over at the statues of her father and mother, knowing that the king and queen of past – their parents – would be proud of their children on this great day.

Krudon and all his evil had been defeated. Bortwig the tree elf was returned to health by the magic of the orb. The wizard Wilzorf had returned to the side of the king, where he rightly belonged, and good reigned over Habilon once again.

As the celebrations roared across the magical land that Josh had made his new home, on the far side, beyond the cherry tree, Claudia Pennington excused herself from her dinner guests to answer a knock on the door of Cherry Tree Manor.

The general was no longer missing!